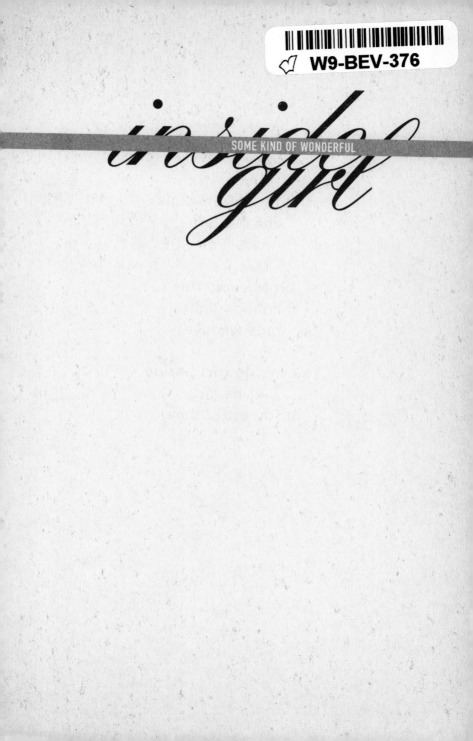

inside girl

SOME KIND OF WONDERFUL

inside girl

SOME KIND OF WONDERFUL

girl

a novel by J. MINTER

author of the insiders

BLOOMSBURY

BLOOMSBURY

Published by Bloomsbury U.S.A. Children's Books
175 Fifth Avenue, New York, NY 10010
Distributed to the trade by Macmillan

Library of Congress Cataloging-in-Publication Data available upon request
ISBN-13: 978-1-59990-165-7 • ISBN-10: 1-59990-165-X

alloy**entertainment**
Produced by Alloy Entertainment
151 West 26th Street, New York, NY 10001

First U.S. Edition 2008
Printed in the U.S.A. by Quebecor World Fairfield
10 9 8 7 6 5 4 3 2 1

All papers used by Bloomsbury U.S.A. are natural, recyclable products
made from wood grown in well-managed forests. The manufacturing
processes conform to the environmental regulations of the country of origin.

to the **OBLC,**
for doing what you do

Chapter 1

*L*ike it or not, my life changes fast.

Last week I was rocking the Cinderella-sans-curfew look at my sister's surprise Halloween bash and I was as happy as I've ever known how to be. I wasn't expecting to come home to such a party, and I definitely wasn't expecting to end up in the arms of Prince Charming—my brand-new, indestructible, quarterback boyfriend, Adam, at the evening's finale.

But the glass slipper had to come off, and soon I was back in my Michael Kors equestrian-style boots with my feet planted a little too firmly on the ground. Stuyvesant High School ground—and I was deep in the heart of final exam freak-out-ville.

Welcome to hell.

"Flan! Flan! Over here! Whoops!"

That was my friend Meredith calling my name as she tripped out of the school entranceway Thursday

1

afternoon. Mer and our other friend Judith have been attached at the dark-wash belt loops since they bought their first matching pair of Mavi jeans in kindergarten. When we all became public school junkies this fall, we took each other under our respective wings. Today, with her curly brown hair springing as she trooped down the stairs, Meredith was half-hidden by a large white pashmina, and she looked like she'd actually sprouted a pair of real wings.

"Hey, girl," I said as we air kissed. "What's with the Cupid duds?"

"I've been looking all over for you," she said, out of breath. "What do you think?"

As Meredith twirled around me, I noticed that the inside of her ivory pashmina had been embroidered with all sorts of sparkly silver stitches. When she held out her arms and gave me a big cherubic grin, she really did resemble an angel.

"I love it," I said, although I was a little confused. "What . . . uh . . . what is it?"

"It's my final exam for my design class. I really want your opinion. Tell me the truth—do you seriously love it?"

I fingered the cashmere shawl and held it up to the light. In the mid-November dusk, it practically glowed.

But even though the stitchwork was amazing, the sleek white pashmina didn't strike me as something that screamed Meredith. In fact, it looked more like something I'd find in the closet of one of my old friends from Miss Mallard's Day—during my former life, as I sometimes thought of it. A life full of ritzy parties, famous boyfriends who wore more expensive jeans than I did, and girls who wouldn't be caught dead sporting the same Chloé sweater twice in one semester.

Meredith couldn't be more different from those girls. She's an *über*-talented seamstress and an accessories guru, but her style is a lot more boho chic— flowing patchwork skirts she makes herself and usually far more bangle bracelets than any girl should wear all at once. But that's one of the things that first drew me to her—she has an uncanny ability to pull off her crazy fashion inspirations. Since both her mom and her grandma work at their own clothing store in the Village, Meredith has pretty much been groomed to have an awesome eye for design.

I handed the masterpiece back to her.

"It's ethereal," I pronounced. "You'll totally ace the class. But you don't need me to tell you that." In fact, I was a little surprised that Meredith was coming to me for fashion advice at all. It had taken me until third period this morning to realize that the Levi's I'd tugged on today were suddenly about three inches too short. And believe me, I'm *so* not the girl to introduce the ankle-length-trouser-cut look.

"Actually," Meredith said, "I do need your opinion. The assignment was to design something for Cecily Brown. Her assistant is going to review our pieces and she might even pick one design from our class to incorporate into CB's spring collection. The proceeds would go to the charity of the winner's choice. Do you know how awesome it would be to have the sales of my pashmina go to Make-A-Wish? With CB's blessing?"

I smiled. Leave it to Meredith to be down-to-earth enough to care more about charity than celebrity. My new friends at Stuy were such a breath of fresh air. True, Meredith, Judith, and I had already had our share of drama over a boy (confession: they'd both had their eye on Adam before I accidentally fell for him), but that felt like ages ago. Okay, so it was only three weeks ago, and maybe the wounds were still a *teensy* bit fresh. But every clique is allowed a little bit of growing pains, right? Plus, standing here with Meredith, I could already feel the stitches that held our friendship together falling back into place. It was so important to me that things between us got back to the way they'd been in the good old days of early fall. I looped my arm through Meredith's and started to walk her toward her train.

"So," Meredith continued, "since I know that your fam is totally in with CB, you're the only one whose opinion I can trust."

I sighed. Scratch what I said before—sometimes my Stuy friends were just as into all the socialite hype as my private school friends were.

"Meredith," I said. "My family isn't really *in* with CB."

"Whatever," she laughed. "She lives down the street from you! *And* Rachel McHenry totally came to your sister's pool party in September *and* you two were wearing the same bathing suit!"

I cringed when I remembered showing up at Feb's benefit party in the same forest green Gucci racer-back two-piece as Rachel McHenry. It was bad enough feeling like I could barely fit into the thing— which I'd tried on at Bendel's just two months before—but to be such a blatant target for mega-star body comparisons . . . I spent the whole party sweating through my YSL cover-up in shame.

"Mer, just because Cecily Brown and Rachel McHenry were in *Wars of Our Mothers* together doesn't mean they share the same fashion brain. And that was my sister's party, which I had nothing to do with. Anyway, that's not even the point. The point isn't what I think Cecily Brown will like, the point is that you're proud of your work. And you are, right?" I said, adjusting the strap of my hobo bag as we crossed Sixth Avenue. "Anyway, it's making me really jealous that you've already finished one final project. I'm one hundred percent going to fail bio this semester."

"You always say that," Meredith said. "And then somehow you ace every test. I don't know how you keep up with school, your wild lifestyle, *and* having a boyfriend."

I sighed and smelled the tough rush of New York all around us. There it was, that little edge in her voice that bordered on passive-aggressive. I was about to open my mouth to argue that she was mistaken about my wild lifestyle, which had recently consisted of mostly studying, studying, and okay, *occasionally* taking a study break to grab a quick ice cream with Adam. But before I could defend myself, Mer flashed her yellow MetroCard at me in good-bye.

"Call me later?" she yelled as she disappeared into the underbelly of Manhattan. "Thanks for your CB insight!"

I was left alone, half-chuckling on the corner of West Fourth. Sometimes it felt like Meredith thought I had a toy chest full of movie stars at home that I took out and played with every night.

I started to make my way home, winding my way through the streets of the West Village. Fall was totally the best time of year to wander around in New York City. All the ginkgo trees were full and hanging low over the zigzagging downtown streets. Every block I turned down today had a new scent: the cheesy deliciousness of John's Pizza on Bleecker; the new perfume wafting out of L'Occitane; the sharp, sweet scent of someone's fire escape barbecue.

I was about to turn down Perry Street when I felt my iPhone buzz in my bag. I fished it out and saw the lit-up JPEG of my mom standing atop Mount Kilimanjaro that my dad had taken on one of their recent jet-setting jaunts.

"Hi, Mom," I said into the phone.

"Flan, darling. You're taking Home Ec this semester, aren't you?" My mother always sounded a little breathless on the phone, but today she was practically panting.

"Um, I don't think Stuy has taught Home Ec since 1957," I said. "Why? What's up?"

I paused at my street corner to read a sign for a

stoop sale on MacDougal Street this weekend. Ooh, hopefully it would be my crazy Peruvian neighbor who made those handblown glass earrings. I'd have to remember to tell Meredith about it.

"Oh, Flan," my mother said, coughing. "It's just that . . . I had a little disaster in the kitchen."

"Mom," I said, stifling a laugh, "did you bake?"

I shuddered to think back to a couple of months ago, when Feb had caught the Martha Stewart bug and had become bent on serving me three hot—if inedible—meals a day for a week. At least I could count on the fact that Mom wouldn't find Feb's since-discarded stash of Anthropologie aprons. My mother rarely strayed from her typical uniform: a black Prada pantsuit and her Hearts On Fire diamonds.

Usually my mother only opened the oven in our professional grade kitchen to look for a place to store another pair of shoes. And she was so rarely in the city that when she was home, she mostly just liked to veg out and watch bad reality TV in our home theater. I wondered what could have possessed her to decide to cook something.

"Well," she continued, "there's no use crying over burned . . . whatever this is. What do you say the two of us pop over to The Little Owl for an early dinner so I can let this place air out?"

I grinned. I adored The Little Owl. "You should burn dinner more often," I said. "See you there in a few."

Normally I wouldn't think twice about meeting my mother at one of her favorite neighborhood haunts for an impromptu dinner out, but as I backtracked to Grove Street, I remembered the conversation I'd had today over a sashimi lunch with Meredith and Judith. Judith was lamenting the fact that she'd been scouring opentable.com for weeks, trying to get a reservation at The Little Owl for her father's birthday, but the place was interminably booked.

I had swallowed my bite of seaweed salad and opened my mouth to say that my mother's college roommate was the owner's wife, and that he'd even come to our house to cook us dinner a few times. I knew I could get Judith a reservation without batting an eye. But sometimes my friends could get either googly-eyed or intimidated when I mentioned a connection to anything they found remotely glamorous. So I ended up keeping my mouth shut. As I sat there, though, the words felt heavy inside me. Friends were supposed to help each other out. What was my problem? I now promised myself that I would mention it to her tomorrow and see if I could hook her up.

I stopped in front of the restaurant to wait for my

mother to arrive, but before I could make a note in my Kate Spade planner, she came up behind me and threw her thin arms around me in a big hug. I grinned and hugged her back. It was always so good to see my mom, especially when she was returning from a long vacation abroad—which was pretty much all the time.

My parents were professional globe-trotters—a trait that both of my siblings seemed to have inherited, because neither of them felt the need to come home more than once a month to recharge their batteries. They all made fun of me constantly for being the homebody nerd in the family. But I didn't care—I loved being home. I loved the balcony window from my bedroom and the view of the brownstone recently bought by my crazy best friend and teen movie star idol, Sara-Beth Benny. I'd gotten used to spending a lot of time on my own, but home was always more homey when my lovably crazy family was around.

"Darn your father," my mother said as she steered me into the restaurant. The place was so tiny that it could only hold about thirty people. The décor was comfortable and pretty simple, with small vases of wildflowers dotting the white tables, and everyone agreed that the food was some of the best in the city. It was still pretty early, so the crowd was kind of quiet, but I knew that by the time we left, the restaurant would be bumping. We took our usual seats at the bench table in the back corner.

"What'd Dad do this time?" I played along. She and my dad loved to antagonize each other. I think getting pissy only to kiss and make up was kind of their shtick. It was cute, I guess, that they still acted like some of the love-struck couples I saw in the halls at Stuy every day. But sometimes I wondered if I was the only grown-up in the Flood family.

"He promises me he'll be home for dinner, so I order this whole lovely meal from FreshDirect." She paused to open the menu. "Ooh, they have those good scallops today. Anyway, then he calls to say there's too much Hamptons traffic to make it back into the city after his golf game. I told him to take the helicopter, but he just won't listen to reason. I was so flustered about it that I skipped straight out to Aveda and made Janice squeeze me in for a detoxifying facial. I completely forgot that I'd left the oven on with the meatloaf inside it, and—"

"Well, your pores are absolutely invisible," I said, giving my mom's hand a squeeze. Even when she's being manic, it's nice to have my mom around. I never know when I'm going to come home to an empty house and a Post-it note with the phone number for my parents' hotel room in Dubai or Maui or

Bali, so I try to cherish every mother-daughter moment I can.

"Thank you, darling. Your pores are lovely too. You must have gotten them from your father, the golf-playing slob. Now, do you want to share the pork chop again? Or should we get the fantastic lobster risotto? What am I talking about? You're a growing girl—you probably want your own dish." She turned to the waiter. "We can't decide. Tell Joey just to give us a little bit of everything."

As my mother nibbled on tiny bites of scallop and I pigged out on the incredible cheesy risotto, we fell into a conversation that was heavier than the meatloaf my mom had burned to a crisp back at home. I was suddenly shocked. My mother wanted to talk about *school*? Could I be hearing correctly?

"Are you happy there? That's all I want to know. Do you think the people are, you know, enough like us?"

"I am happy," I said, glancing behind me to read the dessert menu specials. I was psyched to see that they had my favorite bread pudding tonight. "The classes are actually challenging, and I like that. I also like that the people *aren't* exactly like me. Everyone's down-to-earth. It's refreshing."

"Refreshing is a week at Spa Montage in Laguna,

Flan," my mother said, dabbing her lips with her napkin. "I worry about you. I want to make sure you have all the same opportunities your brother and sister had, the same opportunities I had. You know how much I loved Thoney."

My mother never ceases to regale us with tales of her wild days at her ultra-glitzy alma mater, the all-girls high school I would have attended if I hadn't made the gut-wrenching decision to make a fresh start at Stuyvesant. No one in my family could understand how anything that had happened to me in seventh grade could be so scarring that I'd want to subject myself to public school. But it was a choice I'd made myself, and I was proud of all the things I'd had to overcome since I started school in September.

"I know you did, Mom," I said, as the waiter set down a fantastic-looking plate of bread pudding. "But I love Stuyvesant. My friends are so cool. I totally made the right choice." But as I said those words aloud, I couldn't help but wonder if they were completely true. Sometimes I *wasn't* sure I'd made the right decision. Like when I held things back about myself with my very best friends. I glanced at my mom, who was watching me carefully, and I had the very uncomfortable notion that she might actually be able to read my mind.

"Well, that brings us to our next important topic of conversation," my mother said, eyeing me as I used the biscotti that came with her espresso to sop up some of my caramel sauce. "The Zumbergs have invited us—"

I groaned audibly. *The Zumbergs have invited us* was never an auspicious beginning to a sentence. They were the most intense socialites of all my parents' friends. I got a headache just trying to keep up with my parents' stories of traveling with them. Dinner with the Pacinos, a safari with Karl Lagerfeld—the list went on and on.

"Don't groan. We're all taking an island getaway. The Zumbergs have arranged a fabulous trip to Nevis. They've booked bungalows for fifty people all along the beach! Why don't you bring one of your new friends and we can all get to know each other better in paradise? It's exactly our kind of Thanksgiving, Flan," she said, flashing me a grin. "No cooking!"

"You're right." I had to agree, spearing the last of the bread pudding and imagining myself zoning out on the beach, without a scarf and hat and gloves for a change. "It sounds great."

"Then it's settled. Good Lord, Flan, did you finish that entire dessert already? I knew you'd grown since I last saw you, and now I can see why."

"What do you mean?" I asked. She'd only been gone a few weeks. How could I have grown that much?

She stood up and pushed in her chair. "Come on, Flan, *Idol* comes on in twenty minutes. I haven't seen it since Jennifer Hudson was eliminated." She stopped. "Flan, you're a giant!"

"Mom!" I said.

"It's just, I was so distracted by the kitchen disaster before. Now that I'm looking at you standing, you've shot up like a beanstalk. You must be what, five-foot ten?"

"Mom, I'm five-foot seven."

"*I'm* five-foot seven. You, dear, are now at least three inches taller than me. Don't stop growing either, Flanny. You'll be a model yet! So long and lean. *That* I know you inherited from my side."

But I didn't feel like a model. Looking down at my feet, which suddenly looked really far away, I felt like a stork in too-short jeans. I couldn't believe I hadn't noticed this before. And suddenly, as I followed my mom out of the restaurant, I started to worry. If I couldn't even figure out why none of my clothes seemed to fit anymore, how could I trust myself to make major life decisions about what school, what friends, and what life was best for me?

Chapter 2

DOWN THE RABBIT'S HOLE

The next day after school, Judith and I were hanging at Alice's Tea Cup, waiting for Meredith to join us. Alice's Tea Cup is this fantastic café on the Upper West Side where the pastries are to die for and the décor rule of thumb is that anything goes as long as it's pink and plucked from some shabby chic antique store in the city. Gathering here was one of our standard Friday unwinding rituals.

We always sat at the middle table, right in the center of all the action. We debriefed each other on the week that had passed and planned fun outings for the weekend ahead. At the beginning of the year, when there were tons of new boys at Stuy to discuss, evaluate, and prioritize, we spent so much time talking about guys that Meredith started calling our meetings at the café "Boy Circle," and the name just stuck.

Usually, I really looked forward to Boy Circle. But

16

today, instead of chilling out and enjoying my favorite Rooibos tea blend while we waited for Mer to arrive so we could dish, I felt more like I was having an Alice in Wonderland moment of my own.

For one thing, Judith kept muttering about Meredith's "perpetual inability to arrive anywhere on time." If she'd been wearing a top hat instead of her woven lavender wool beret, I might have mistaken her for the Mad Hatter. Even her standard hair flipping habit had been aggravated by Meredith's tardiness, and I was trying to stay out of range of her flying blond locks. She was wearing a white oxford shirt, and a cute little blue tie peaked out of her Bendel's cashmere V-neck. The whole women-wearing-tailored-men's-clothing trend was practically created for Judith.

"You know," she said, straightening her tie, "this is just like Meredith. To go on a date last night and then be late for Boy Circle today! Doesn't she know she's torturing us?"

Not wanting to side with her or against her, I kept my eyes on the menu.

"Mmm-hmm," I said jokingly. "The nerve of that girl. So what are we going to eat?"

I was still recovering from the night before when my mother had called attention to my major growth spurt. Sure, *she* still thought it was fabulous. *Don't stop wearing heels, Flan,* she'd told me when she saw me in flip-flops at the breakfast table. *There's nothing more showstopping than a tall woman in stilettos.*

It didn't help that Judith was the definition of petite or that everyone else in the café seemed to be a six-year-old at a birthday party. Happy little girls in pink tiaras paraded around us, making me feel like I'd just swallowed the *Eat Me* petit four from Alice in Wonderland and blown up to the size of a house.

My stomach growled. It hadn't been that long since I'd had lunch, but I was famished. I sighed and decided to embrace my growth spurt by just indulging in Alice's awesome fried chicken with a Shirley Temple to wash it down.

"You're late," Judith said, as Meredith came in and made her way toward our table.

"Yeah, yeah, I know," Meredith said. "For a very important date."

She piled her stuff on top of Judith's giant North Face backpack and my Brooklyn Industries messenger bag. Meredith always carted around several bags. As scattered as she could be, she was super anal about her art supplies. There were different colored totes for her knitting yarns, her jewelry supplies, and, occasionally, her schoolbooks.

"Sorry, I had to stop by Pearl Art Supplies for these awesome new beads." Meredith held out her new baubles for us to admire. She cradled them carefully, as if she were holding the Hope Diamond. But they were black and tan wood and kind of weird looking. Judith and I both did our best *oh, interesting* coos and smiles.

"Speaking of important dates," I said to Meredith as she tucked her beads away. "What's new in the world of you and Jules? Did you end up going to Bowlmor last night?"

"Yes!" Judith said, like she'd been waiting her whole life to make that exclamation. "I'm going through a major gossip drought. Spill all your bowling escapades ASAP. And please don't tell me Jules brought his own bowling shoes."

Jules was a friend of my ex-boyfriend Bennett, whom Meredith had liked just before—and then again after—she started obsessing over Adam. I was particularly interested in the details of their date because the fact that Meredith's mind was occupied with thoughts of Jules and his fedoras made me feel a tiny bit less guilty about Adam.

But Meredith just shrugged and folded her pink napkin into a tiny triangle. "I dunno. He's just kind of . . . goofy. There's something about a guy with a hat collection. . . ."

Judith held up a finger. "Excuse me," she said. "Are you or are you not the girl who darted into the janitor's closet recently because you were so intimidated by the beauty of a particular beanie of his?"

We all cracked up and then Meredith sighed.

"Yeah, I think we're just going to be friends. Last night we didn't have anything to talk about except why the best bowling shirts have stripes. Besides, there's only room for so many hair accessories in one relationship. And I'm not giving up my headbands." Meredith adjusted the polka-dot strip of fabric she'd woven expertly through her bun. Then she tucked a loose brown ringlet behind her ear. "In other news," she said, leaning forward in her chair with a mischievous look. "Any recent run ins with the Kelvinator to report, Judith?"

Judith groaned. Kelvin was this super creepy guy who had the hots for her. The time and energy she'd spent warding him off was equal only to the time and energy she put into her science fair project last month.

"Don't even bring him up during Boy Circle!" Judith said, blushing and covering her ears. "Remember how I accidentally flirted with him because he was cruelly disguised as a frog to throw me off?"

"Judith," I laughed, "the costume wasn't a ploy to

trick you into flirting with him. It was Halloween! But yes, I do remember."

"Well," Judith said, going for the double hair flip, "yesterday I was looking at his Facebook page, and he has a picture of me up there! Isn't that like some sort of identity theft?"

"I think what we need to revisit is the fact that you're admittedly cruising Kelvin's Facebook page," Meredith said, nudging me. "Care to explain that one, Judith?"

"Ooh, busted. You totally love Kelvin," I said, laughing.

As I looked at my friends across the table, I realized that, despite Judith's earlier impatience, it was almost better to hold out on spilling our gossip for these Friday afternoon sessions. The payoff was so worth the wait.

"If you guys say the name Kelvin one more time, I might lose my appetite. Anyway, the person we really need to hear from is you, Flan. Don't you have something special planned with Adam this weekend? For your *anniversary*?"

I blushed and cleared my throat. I guessed it was only a matter of time before the Boy Circle wand landed on me, but it still made me uncomfortable to talk to the 'diths about Adam. I tried to stall, glancing across the restaurant, where everyone was singing "Happy Birthday." A chic Upper East Side mother was cutting a giant pink cake for her daughter. She could have used the same frosting-coated knife to cut the insta-tension between Mer, Judith, and me. Why did I feel like their eyes were suddenly boring into me? Was I just being totally paranoid? I would have given anything to be that little girl, blowing out my candles and wishing for a time when my friends didn't have even the smallest reason—though they swore they were over it—to resent me.

Not too long ago, I'd been the one making *them* agree to the No Adam Rule when they both simultaneously started crushing on him at the beginning of the year. At the time, I was just taking preventative measures to avoid a toxic situation. I couldn't have my only two friends at school fighting over the same guy!

But then, I went and did the worst thing that a friend could ever do.

I fell for him myself.

The truth was, it happened so slowly, I didn't even see it coming. For a while, I'd mistaken Adam for just my obnoxious lab partner. I thought he only cared about making lewd remarks in class for the benefit of his meathead friends at the back of the room.

I used to dread biology—having to hear all those testosterone-induced grunts from behind me.

But then, when we were assigned to monitor a frog together, I learned how funny and down-to-earth he was. And he was so cute and parental about our little Bogie. I was dating someone else at the time, so Adam was not even on my radar—at least not in that way.

But by now, we'd been going strong for almost a month. We did have an anniversary coming up, but everything was still just uncomfortable enough with Meredith and Judith that I didn't feel like talking about the fact that Adam had promised to take me to Perilla in the West Village for a romantic dinner tomorrow night. I'd been dying to go there ever since Harold, the owner, won Season One of *Top Chef*. Judith and I had been watching the reruns together on Bravo and I knew, under normal circumstances, she'd be psyched that I was finally going to eat there. But something made me hold back. And it was all this *holding back* that was really starting to freak me out. I thought of my mom grilling me at dinner last night and I started to turn red.

It was kind of awful having to worry that an inno-cent discussion at Boy Circle could turn into a *The Hills*–style standoff in no time.

"Um, so, what's everyone doing for Thanksgiving?" I asked innocently.

"My grandma's burning a turkey again," Meredith sighed, pouring us all more tea. "It's tradition."

"Boo," Judith said as she popped a raspberry petit four into her mouth. "My parents are going to visit my sister at her study-abroad program in Budapest. They're chucking me off to my aunt's house in rural Pennsylvania for the week. Did I mention that I'm dreading it?"

"Go ahead, Flan," Mer said. "Torture us with your special plans."

Judith laughed. "Yeah, what is it? A banquet at the Hiltons' house? Dinner at the Rainbow Room? Or will you be pigging out on wasabi rice crisps and crazily expensive champagne with Sara-Beth Benny?" She flicked her hair around, and this time a lock actually hit my cheek.

My face burned. Meredith and Judith had made remarks like this in the past about SBB, but they were always said in good humor. Today, because I still had the awkward Adam moment on my mind, I wasn't so sure.

"Actually," I mumbled, looking down at my empty plate, "we're taking a trip to Nevis with some of our family friends. As if my mom needs another

Caribbean vacation. Anyway . . . I was going to . . . I'm allowed to invite one of you to come with."

Meredith's jaw dropped. Judith's fork clattered to her plate. They stared at me in stunned silence.

"Omigod!"

"Flan!"

"You have to take me!"

"My Thanksgiving is going to suck so much more than hers!"

"Not even! Have you ever *been* to rural Penn-sylvania?"

"I'll do *anything*!"

They were talking so fast, I could barely keep up. Suddenly both my friends were leaning across the table, all eager smiles and sparkling eyes. Even the little kids in the restaurant were looking at us.

"Well," I said slowly, glad to see that they were so into the idea, but slightly overwhelmed by their exuberance. "I don't know . . . how am I supposed to decide?"

"I'll do your bio homework for a month," Judith threw out.

"Flan doesn't need help with her homework," Meredith said, grabbing a piece of frilly fabric from one of her bags. "I can add an awesome ruffled hem to the bottom of your skirt so it won't be so short on you."

"Hey!" I said, looking down at my plum corduroy Alice + Olivia skirt. Well, maybe it *had* gotten a little too short.

Judith laid her hand on mine. "I like the way your skirt looks, Flan. Plus, I know a sophomore girl who's an office aide. I can get you a *permanent* hall pass."

Meredith leaned back in her chair and crossed her arms over her chest. She looked like she was about to lay down her trump card.

"I promise to lose any last bit of a grudge that I might have about"—she paused dramatically—"Adam."

Our table was quiet for a moment.

Then Judith said, "So will I."

"You guys," I said.

"No, seriously," Meredith said, and Judith nodded. "It's time we put all of this mess behind us . . . in Nevis!"

Wow. At least I wasn't the only one who still felt like Adam was the eight-hundred-pound quarterback in the room that none of us wanted to talk about. I guess we were on the same page, which was such a huge relief. I couldn't help it—my lips curled up in a grin.

"You know what," I told them, "screw the Zumbergs. If they have enough room for fifty people in their bungalows, they can make room for fifty-one. I really want both of you to come."

At that instant, the whole restaurant erupted in cheers. The bratty six-year-old had finally unwrapped her last massive pink-ribboned box (another life-size American Girl doll), and all the other parents seemed to be celebrating the fact that the party was over. More immediately, at our table, Meredith and Judith had both attacked me. They flung a tangle of arms around my shoulders, ruffled my ponytail, and even kissed my forehead. You'd think I had just asked them to be the maids of honor in my wedding.

"Oh, Flan," Judith breathed. "You won't regret this."

"We are going to have *somuchfun*," Meredith agreed.

And suddenly, I couldn't wait to be on the beach with them. I could picture the three of us lying out on matching plush terrycloth towels, rotating the direction of our chaise lounges in time with the sun. I'd pour drinks from a frosty pitcher of virgin daiquiris, Meredith would do all our hair up in crazy twists and knots, and Judith would follow us around with sunscreen. And the tropical sun would set on any unpleasant misunderstandings we'd had in the past.

"Just so you know," Judith said, shaking me out of

my reverie. "I would have totally killed you if you'd picked Meredith over me."

We all laughed, but as I looked across the table, my stomach knotted. As SBB always wisely told me—that girl has a proverb for everything—every jest carries a glimmer of truth.

*O*n Saturday night, I was standing before my vanity mirror, trying to figure out how to zip up the back of my new black knee-length dress, when Adam called to say he'd be at my place in twenty minutes. I calmly said I couldn't wait to see him, and then flipped into frantic primp mode.

I wished Feb were home. I'd been her date prep assistant since I was seven years old and she went on her very first official date. His name was Trenton Tallard the Third, and he asked Feb to accompany him to his sister's wedding. I still remember the pink streaks she put in her hair and the fishnets she insisted on wearing, despite my mother's stern warning that "no respectable girl goes to Tavern on the Green dressed like Gwen Stefani." I sat next to Feb in front of her vanity while she painted both sets of our toenails with dark green NARS nail polish.

Whenever I had trouble sleeping when I was a little kid, I used to imagine my own first date. I'd lie in bed and picture my own grown-up self, sitting in front of my vanity, switching the lighting setting to *evening* and primping and powdering so that my own Prince Charming would be blown away when he knocked on my front door with calla lilies.

Little did I know then that the ideal date in a guy's universe didn't exactly include an arranged bouquet from Michael George and a carriage ride through Central Park. So far, I'd had my share of boyfriends, but Jonathan's idea of eighth grade courtship included buying me a large box of Hot Tamales and coming over with something from Netflix. And Bennett, my most recent ex, was very sweet, but his romantic overtures included me helping him leaf through racks of comic books in dusty comic book shops in the Village.

Adam was different. He was super observant, so he was great at reading me and was always the first person to notice the little things—from a new haircut I'd gotten, to my embarrassing fear of cactuses, to the face I unintentionally made when I was ready to leave a party.

Which is why it didn't surprise me that Adam actually remembered the date of our one-month anniversary, *and* thought to plan ahead since it fell during

Thanksgiving weekend, *and* showed up on time with a bouquet of some really unique bright orange calla lilies.

"Hey, Flan," he said, when I pulled open the front door. I loved that when he talked to me, his voice sounded totally different than it did when I heard him calling out football plays on the field. "You look really nice," he said.

"Thanks," I said. It still made me blush when he complimented me, but suddenly I was glad I'd done more than just slick on some ChapStick and throw on a pair of jeans like I usually did when we hung out. I'd actually gotten a manicure at Bliss that morning, and I used the good Frédéric Fekkai hair mask, too. The dress I was wearing (I'd finally managed to zip it up) was from 202, which is probably my favorite store in the city. It's a trendy brunch spot slash chic clothing store. You can gorge yourself on lemon ricotta pancakes and not even have to leave your seat to do some of the best window-shopping in Chelsea.

"Ready to go?" Adam asked.

I nodded and turned around to give my Pomeranian, Noodles, one last kiss.

"Be good," I told Noodles, who sneezed out a good-bye.

We were halfway down the stairs of my brownstone when we noticed my parents walking up the sidewalk.

"Who are these two trendsetters?" my dad asked, jokingly. He'd already met Adam—they'd spent a good twenty minutes comparing their fantasy football teams, which was the ultimate icebreaker with my dad.

"Hello, Mr. and Mrs. Flood," Adam said, smiling easily. It was cool that he never got high-strung about being around my parents.

"Flan, you're a goddess," my mother said. "How did I ever give birth to you?"

It was the same thing my mother said every time she was home to see me, whether I was wearing a prom dress or pajamas.

As we said good-bye to my parents and started walking to the restaurant, Adam put his arm around my shoulders. Even though it was kind of heavy, I appreciated the gesture to shield me from the icy November wind. Walking next to Adam, I realized I was glad that I'd decided to go with the vintage red heels instead of my typical Hollywould flats. I had been feeling like the Tower of Pisa this week, but then I remembered with relief that Adam was six–foot four. It was the first time all week that I hadn't felt like a giant.

When we got to Perilla, we were seated at one of the

curved banquettes. The place was laid out really nicely, with lots of bold reds and whites and dark woods. The music was on pretty loudly and there was an even louder buzz of voices talking over it. I had to scrunch really close to Adam to get him to hear me when I talked, which wasn't a bad thing at all.

Over appetizers of duck meatballs, Adam took my hand. "I owe you an apology," he said.

"For what?" I asked. What could he possibly have done wrong?

"For being so insanely busy with football. I know I haven't had a ton of time to hang out. But between Coach pressuring me to implement all these new plays and double practices . . . well, I just hope these past few weeks haven't been too hard on you."

I was on my way to laughing out loud when I realized that Adam was being one hundred percent serious. *Uh-oh.* Was it bad that I'd barely noticed how swamped he'd been with football? "Don't sweat it," I said. "I've been crazy busy myself."

"But Flan, you deserve a guy who can totally be there for you. As soon as football season's over next month, I'm going to bring the focus back to us."

"Oh," I said. "Okay."

The truth was, I was happy with the way our relationship was going. I mean, we already saw each other every day at school, and we hung out at least once a week. How much more did he think we were missing out on? As Adam snuggled closer to me in our curved leather banquette and kissed my cheek, I suddenly found myself wondering whether I was ready for him to *bring the focus back to us*.

I tried to lighten the mood. "So guess where I'm going for Thanksgiving break?" I asked.

"Plymouth Rock?" Adam joked.

"Not quite," I said. "My family's going to some bungalow resort in Nevis. I'm super excited. Meredith and Judith are coming, too."

"My family's going to Chicago," Adam said. "We go to the Bears game every year. It's fun—not Nevis fun, but still pretty awesome."

He refilled my water glass from the crystal pitcher on the table. "So, how are Judith and Meredith? Everything back to normal between you guys after . . ." His voice trailed off. He knew we'd gotten in a little tiff over him, but I'd tried to spare him most of the gory details.

"Completely," I said as the waiter set down our steaming entrees. I couldn't wait to dig into my organic free-range chicken with baby bok choy. "They're such great girls—nothing like my old friends from Miss Mallard's."

Adam squinted at me and angled his head. "What do you mean? What were your old friends like?"

I didn't know why I'd brought that up. The memories of my old friends must have been all tangled up in my head with the thoughts my mother planted about returning to the private school world. I thought of one girl's face in particular: Kennedy Pearson, with her cascade of wavy dark hair and piercing green eyes. She'd been one of many Queen Bees at Miss Mallard's and, once upon a time, we'd been friends.

But that was a long time ago, and right now I was with down-to-earth, sweet Adam, who didn't need to know a thing about the awfulness that was Kennedy Pearson.

"Just, um, not as cool," I said. "Everyone I've met at Stuy has been so chill and nice and fun to be around." I gave him my brightest, happiest picture-taking smile. "Especially you."

As soon as we polished off our main courses, I had my eye on the dessert list—I never feel like a meal is over until I've gorged myself on something like . . . sticky pineapple coconut cake. *Yum*.

When Adam saw me ogling the dessert menu, he said, "Oh . . . I was thinking of showing you this amazing ice cream place I'd just discovered on Bleecker, but if you'd rather stay here, that's fine, too."

Immediately, I knew what place he was talking about. Cones—the place that had been my favorite ice cream spot for years, the place I'd discovered when Jonathan took me there in eighth grade. Jonathan, who, unlike Adam, actually knew about a good spot before the whole planet read about it on Citysearch. I shook myself out of that thought. A heads-up on the new hot spots was *not* the reason I was dating Adam. I was done with guys like Jonathan.

"On second thought," Adam said, "let's just stay here. From the way you're staring down the table next to us, it looks like you've got your heart set on the cake they ordered."

I laughed. "Am I that easy to read?"

"I like to pay attention," he said, looking at me earnestly, like he was ready to bring the focus back to us *right now*.

"Well, I don't mess around when it comes to coconut," I said lightly, examining my dessert fork to avoid his intense gaze.

After we polished off our amazing cake, Adam paid the bill and started to walk me home. Just then, out of the corner of my eye, I spotted some of the boys from Feb and Patch's crew walking across the street, probably headed out for steaks at Freeman's. Of course, they were dressed to impress, every one of them sporting three-hundred-dollar jeans and a watch the size of a hockey puck.

They all had tons of product in their hair so they were practically glinting, and sure, more than a few of them were shorter than me by now, but there was still something about the way they sauntered down Bleecker Street like they owned it. It made me shiver.

There were guys in this crowd I used to drool over, and now here I was, walking on the other side of the street encased by my all-American football player. For a second, I felt like I was living in *Grease,* a real-life Sandra Dee running into the T-Birds at the diner with my clean-cut athlete boyfriend.

Suddenly Arno Wildenburger caught my eye. It was the first time I'd seen him in forever without giant Gucci sunglasses protecting his face. Tonight, they rested on top of his head—in case he needed them in the dimly lit club, I was sure. As we approached each other, Arno's mouth curled into a smile and I was sure my cover was blown. Soon all the boys would be hooting about Patch's little sister on a date.

But then, something strange happened. Arno winked at me. And I realized it wasn't because he recognized me—he didn't. *Arno was checking me out?*

I ducked my head into Adam's shoulder, hoping this would keep me out of sight from the others.

Luckily, Adam didn't seem to notice anything strange and had enough to say about football until we turned the corner. Maybe he would think that when I pulled him closer, I was just impressed by his football stats. Adam just wasn't the type of guy ever to guess that I'd be using him as a bodyguard, a shield against my other life.

When we reached my front stoop, Adam put both his arms around me.

"Thanks for an awesome time tonight," he said.

As he kissed me lightly on the lips, I *should* have been thinking about what a perfect night it had been from start to finish. How chivalrous Adam always was. How great he looked in his preppy tucked-in yellow Brooks Brothers shirt.

But for some reason, I wasn't. I couldn't shake the feeling that something had just shifted inside me. Maybe it had to do with literally hiding behind Adam when I saw Arno & Co.

Was it because I didn't feel like having my date interrupted?

Or was it because it was more than just Adam I was hiding behind? Was my whole switch to Stuy a way of hiding from my other life?

Chapter 4

$\mathcal{I}$'d set my alarm for eight o'clock Sunday morning, knowing that I had a full day of packing ahead of me. If there was one thing in the world that I hated to do, it was to pack. I had a hard enough time deciding what to wear every morning to school—how was I supposed to know what I'd feel like wearing a full week ahead of time?

I would have asked Feb for some help, but we hadn't seen her in two weeks. There'd been one picture of her in Page Six at 5 Ninth with Ric Roderickson's director brother, Kirk, but that was last Thursday and the messages I'd gotten from her cell phone had all been totally garbled. My dad did show me a photo Feb had sent to his iPhone the day before. Feb was wearing a business suit and cat's-eye glasses, sitting in a boardroom next to Emerald Wilcox, daughter of Blast Records music mogul D. Wilcox, and what looked like a team of architects.

"What's she playing this week, do you think?" he asked me, showing the picture.

I shrugged as my mother called out from the terrace, "Maybe she's working on that new Google competition to send a rocket to the moon—I saw a segment on *The Soup*! Check with Patch, he'll know."

But none of us had seen Patch either, ever since he left a week ago to get a burger at Shake Shack and apparently forgot to come back. I wondered if his disappearance had anything to do with the fact that his Princeton early admissions letter arrived two days before he wandered out. But then, it wouldn't be like Patch to worry about the contents of that letter—that would be something *I'd* do. Patch had probably forgotten entirely that this week was the big reveal for early admissions decisions. The letter sat there on our kitchen counter, just chilling out, much like its addressee, calmly wedged between the fake lemons my mother had bought in Brazil that my father thought looked like grenades.

I knew when the time came for *my* college admissions, I'd be chasing the mailman down the block every day after school. I was stressed out enough by the idea of packing for a simple one-week vacation.

Meredith, Judith, and I had scheduled a conference call at ten so we could have a virtual packing pow-wow. As Meredith had wisely informed us, three heads were better than one when it came to limited suitcase space.

When my phone rang, I had to scramble over some piles of clothes on my slate gray canopy bed to answer it. I sat on my favorite Conran Shop rocking chair under the framed (and signed) movie poster from SBB's latest blockbuster hit and was greeted by M&J's chipper voices on the other end of the line.

"Okay, first things first," Meredith said. "Who's bringing their diffuser? I think we only need one."

"What are you talking about?" Judith said, and I figured she was going to make a crack that Meredith's curls were the only things that were going to need diffusing among our three heads. But then she said, "First things first means, how was your date last night, Flan?"

"Well," I said cautiously. This was the first time Adam had come up since the girls had professed that they were over it. I decided to test the waters. "We went to Perilla," I said.

"*Perilla!*" Judith shouted. "You're so lucky! How was it?"

"It was great," I said, already feeling relieved. "And he brought me calla lilies."

"*Calla lilies!*" Meredith said, matching Judith's pitch. "Those are your favorite! He's so sweet!"

It was awesome to hear them both sound genuinely excited for me. I leaned in to smell the lilies in their vase next to my chair.

"Okay, let's cut to the really good part. How was the kiss?" Judith said. She was such a sucker for the good night kiss anecdote.

"Um, *yeah,*" Meredith said. "Get to the good stuff."

"On a scale of one to ten?" I said, fully getting into the storytelling mode. "Eleven. I'd say it was just slightly more passionate than normal, without feeling too intense."

"*Awesome,*" they said simultaneously. What was even more awesome was their reaction to my date. Finally everything was starting to feel back to normal among us.

Judith sighed. "And I thought I was having fun last night watching the DVD of *Weeds* with my boy-friends, Ben and Jerry."

"Hey," Meredith said. "There'll be none of that party pooper-ness in Nevis. Speaking of which, I just had the *most amazing idea*! You might even call it a packing stroke of genius."

"Okay," Judith said. She was used to Mer's bubbly outlook. "Lay it on us."

"What if," Meredith said, "we come up with a set of rules, one for each of us to follow? Our mission is to break out of our normal fashion modes and release our inner vacation goddesses!"

Half an hour later, we'd decided on the rules.

Judith was to bring at least two pairs of shoes that were *not* sensible. If necessary, she was to visit the Barneys warehouse for said non-sensible shoes. Extra points would be awarded for heel height.

Meredith was to try to limit patterned pieces to one per outfit. It was true you could get away with wearing just about anything in the Village, but Mer's bohemian threads, when layered one on top of the other—paisleys and bold flowers and once, I swear, I even spotted argyle in her closet—well, Judith and I worried all that activity just might frighten the natives.

As for me . . . my wardrobe in Nevis could not include more than three solid-colored boat neck shirts—my fallback when I'm feeling drained of fashion energy.

When the vacation attire rules were sufficiently agreed upon and our suitcases were completely stuffed, we hung up and agreed to meet at the Cosi in Terminal D at LaGuardia the next morning.

I was about to close my closet door when I began

to worry that, with only three solid-colored shirts to choose from, I wasn't really bringing the best options. I didn't want to break the rules, but suddenly I wasn't sure whether I should pull the lavender Petit Bateau T-shirt in favor of a cream colored Marc Jacobs tank. I held both of them up against my torso in the mirror. Making all of these decisions was pretty exhausting. Why couldn't I just have it all?

At least I hadn't had to choose between Meredith and Judith on this trip. Friendship was one arena where it never helped to be restrictive.

Suddenly the door to my bedroom burst open and in marched Sara-Beth Benny.

"Omigod! Sara-Beth, you scared me!"

She struck a paparazzi-worthy pose, with one hand on her hip and her chest and butt extended so that she looked even tinier than normal. In her high-pitched voice, she called out, "Get over here and give me a kiss if you want to touch the lips that Jake Riverdale was smooching last night!"

"Would you settle for a big hug?" I laughed.

"That works," she said, embracing me and plopping down on my bed. "Actually, you're right not to be starstruck about JR. I mean yeah, he's gorgeous, but he's actually sort of a moron. It's really extremely unfortunate," she said dramatically.

I knew Sara-Beth was on location somewhere in Texas, starring opposite Jake Riverdale in a remake of *Bonnie and Clyde*. Aside from what she was wearing—a Pucci do-rag, ankle boots, and an oversized jersey knit T-shirt dress—I could totally see how her spark plug energy and dramatic flair would make her a great Bonnie. I envisioned her egging Clyde on to hold up just one more bank before they called it a night.

"Flan, you wouldn't believe the pressure I'm under. I told Spencer and his team I just can't *work* with these people, but they only care about the bottom line. Ugh, agents! You know?"

"I know." I laid down next to SBB on the bed and patted her shoulder, my packing woes forgotten. Sometimes SBB was the only person who could bring me back down to reality. Probably because she was so crazy.

"Sometimes I think I'm the only sane person on the set," she continued. "Ric Roderickson is the director from hell. He listens to anything Jake says. *Bonnie and Clyde* is a *classic*—it is so *not* supposed to be a musical. I swear, if I have to sit through one more table read practically yodeling my lines, I'm going to—" She shot up from my bed and landed on my suitcase. "Wait, Flan, are you going somewhere? And did you grow? You barely even fit on this bed! You promised me you wouldn't get any taller!"

I stood up too and noticed the striking difference between SBB's height and my own. She's very sensitive about her five-foot stature and once made me sign an affidavit saying I wouldn't wear heels in front of her.

"Sorry, SBB, it wasn't really something I could help. Believe me, I wish I wasn't so enormous all of a sudden."

"Enormous schmeenormous. You're just saying that to make me feel better. I was told by Lucy, my tarot reader, that I was going to be five-foot eleven someday. You're so lucky, Flan, you know that? *Sigh*." Her bony shoulders sagged.

"I guess so . . . ," I said.

"I know so and that's that. Now tell me, where are you taking your tall self? Somewhere fabulous, I hope?"

"My family's going to Nevis for Thanksgiving," I said. "We're leaving tomorrow morning."

"Nevis?" SBB jumped up and began to rummage through my sock drawer for no apparent reason. "What I wouldn't give to be back in Nevis! I once spent two of the most amazing weeks in Nevis—now, was that last year or the year before? I can't remem-

ber." She started waltzing around my room with a pair of my tube socks in her hands. "It was perfect. You remember, when I was dating . . . what was his name . . ."

"Jared," I said.

"Jared! That's right, the one who modeled for Calvin Klein for, like, a second. Totally washed up now and it's so sad. The problem was his head, if you remember. It was shaped like, what did I used to say?"

"A cereal box."

SBB collapsed in a fit of giggles, which always made me laugh, too. Being with SBB was always so easy. All we did was make each other laugh. No drama, no competition. It might have been because we existed on totally different planets, but still.

"So you're going to Nevis and this is what you're bringing?" she said, eying my suitcase. I knew what was coming next.

She snatched up the two shirts I'd been deciding on when she first burst into the room. Now they were crumpled into two balls next to my suitcase.

"Didn't I teach you how to fold?" she asked. "My guru taught me. I know, yoga and material objects don't really go hand in hand, but he was really very fashion forward." Sara-Beth whipped the shirts into two origami triangles, each one-eighth its original size, and tucked them both into my suitcase.

"No, wait," I told her, reaching for the shirts. "I'm only allowed to bring three solid-colored boatnecks!"

"What in God's name are you talking about?" she said. "I never want to hear you talk about packing restrictions again. You can never be too prepared in Nevis. Now, what you need is a bigger suitcase. Do you have one lying around someplace? Where's your storage facility? You must have something."

I shook my head.

"Well then, let's say no more," SBB said, spinning around my room. "I have an absolutely genius idea!

*B*efore I knew it, I was in the backseat of an uptown-bound minivan taxi next to SBB. I had to clutch her arm as the cabbie zipped through more than a few red lights in a row while heading north on Sixth Avenue. When we hit a street fair on 23rd Street and the smell of kettle corn and cheap Thai food struck my nose, the cab driver swung a hard right toward Fifth.

"I didn't know you went slumming in cabs," I joked. "Is it Richardo's day off or something?"

"Oh no no no, Flan," she said. "Taxis are the way to go. Much more incognito *and* I love the idea that there's a chance I might get on *Cash Cab* and end up on the Discovery Channel. It'd be so much fun to be on reality TV disguised as someone else. Wouldn't that be hilarious?"

"Hilarious," I agreed. I didn't want to burst SBB's

bubble and tell her that one of Patch's friends worked on the show *Cash Cab* (a game show in which unsuspecting New Yorkers hail cabs only to find a disco-clothes-wearing, trivia-questioning driver inside), so I knew that all of the contestants they picked up were staged. Anyway, she was busy turning incognito, as she almost always does when we go out in public together.

"What should it be today?" she asked, rummaging through the biggest bright green Longchamp tote I'd ever seen. It was easily twice her size.

"What are my options?" I asked.

"Ooh, I have the perfect wig in here for an Upper East Side private school brat," she said, and produced a wig of flowing black waves that looked alarmingly similar to Kennedy Pearson's haircut last year.

"That looks right," I said.

"What else are the girls wearing these days, Flan? You're my link to the *real* people in this town."

I helped SBB sort through a torrent of printed silk shawls and giant belt buckles to accessorize her T-shirt dress. From the bottom of the bag, we picked the biggest pair of sunglasses we could find—red, Alain Mikli—and slapped them on her pretty little face.

"You look like everyone I grew up going to school with," I told her. "I'm a little scared of you, actually."

"Don't be scared, Flan. You just saved my life. Another costuming success!"

I looked down at my own white boatneck shirt and jeans and felt suddenly very un-glamorous. If there was one thing I was not, it was a costuming success.

"Now will you tell me where we're going?" I asked. I wondered if I should have changed, too.

The cab screeched to a halt at 53rd Street and Madison.

"Here!" SBB exclaimed. She paid the driver and pulled me onto the street and then into the high ceilings and bright lights of the Bric's luggage store. The inside of the store was spare and meticulously laid out by color, size, and type of travel. "This is *the* place to buy Nevis-worthy luggage. I wouldn't let you leave home without it," SBB said.

Soon, Sara-Beth was whipping me around the store, pointing out every piece of luggage that she personally owned and every piece of luggage that she'd convinced one of her friends to buy.

"Satisfaction guaranteed!" she grinned, unzipping pockets and showing me the various compartments with a *Deal or No Deal* Girl flourish. "This one's for jewelry, and here's one for your lingerie. There's a climate-controlled compartment in case you have any face creams that need refrigeration. I use this one for fuzzy handcuffs . . . whoops, did I say that?" I tried to stifle my laughter as one of the sales clerks turned to glare at us, but it ended up coming out my nose, which only made SBB more hysterical.

When we'd calmed down, she grabbed my hand. "Ooh, are you bringing Noodles with you?"

I shook my head. "Not this time. He's not much of a jet-setter—the whole air sickness thing. He's staying with Liesel."

"That's too bad, because they have the cutest doggie totes. I bought a couple for myself, just in case I ever stop being terrified of animals."

It was always a blast to shop with SBB, and soon I was totally absorbed in finding the perfect duffel bag for the trip. It was funny—my Tumi rolling suitcase had seemed perfectly fine this morning, but it now felt totally lame in comparison to all of these great new options.

"This one," I said finally, pausing in front of a sleek burgundy duffel with an option for 360-degree rolling. "Perfection."

"Definitely." SBB nodded enthusiastically.

As someone with a track record of terrible decision-making capabilities, I certainly had an easy enough time upgrading my luggage, thanks to Sara-Beth.

"I needed that," I said to SBB as we approached

the register wheeling my new top-of-the-line duffel bag. "I should let you make all my life decisions."

There was a crowd of people in front of us at the register—apparently I wasn't the only one getting outfitted for the Thanksgiving break.

A group of girls turned around as we approached.

"Is that *Flan Flood*?" I heard a voice say.

It was Olivia Quayle, an old friend of mine from Miss Mallard's, whom I hadn't talked to since eighth grade. She'd grown a few inches and maybe had a nose job. She looked a lot more dazzling than I'd remembered. She was wearing a cropped cream-colored wool jacket, and her wavy auburn hair hung down her back. She gave me a bright, genuine smile.

"Hey, Olivia," I said, giving her a kiss. You never greeted anyone from Miss Mallard's with a hug. It was only ever the air-kiss. "Great to see you. You look awesome."

"Oh my God, not even," Olivia said. "*You* look amazing. What model's body did you steal? You're so tall now."

I heard SBB sniff beside me at that comment. It would be polite to introduce her, but she'd kill me if I blew her cover.

"Um, this is my friend . . . Mandy," I said. "She goes to Stuy with me."

"Nice to meet you, Mandy," Olivia said. "And this is Veronica and Dara—new recruits at Thoney this year. They were at Little Red until last year, and we've been BFFs since day one of freshman year. Right, girls?"

Veronica and Dara nodded and grinned, and both of them actually seemed really nice. For a second, I wondered if I would have been in their crew if I'd stuck around and gone to Thoney.

Dara turned to SBB and said, "You look really familiar. Do we know each other from somewhere?"

SBB readjusted her wig and purred in a southern accent I'd never heard before. "I don't see how we could. I've only just moved here from Texas."

Since no one really knew what to say to a girl from Texas, Olivia turned back to me.

"Well, we really miss you, Flan, but we hear through the grapevine that Stuy's going well. Dating the captain of the football team or something?"

I blushed and laughed a little. "Adam," I said. "We just started dating a little while ago, but he's a pretty cool guy." I wondered how they'd found out about my love life. Was it really something people talked about in the Thoney grapevine? It felt sort of nice to think that people were saying I was doing well at Stuyvesant, but I realized that I was much more interested in talking to Olivia about the latest dirt in her circle than I was in talking about Adam.

"Tell me about Thoney. Who's stealing whose boyfriend? Who's getting caught smoking in the bathroom? What are the upperclassmen like? I want to know everything."

The girls giggled and stepped closer to start whispering about school. I was having so much fun that I barely noticed SBB retreating—until I felt one very hard pull on my left hand.

"Oh, sorry, S—Mandy. I got caught up—"

I stopped talking at the sight of SBB's face, which had turned as pale as a ghost.

"Are you okay?" I asked.

"Too many people," she whispered, robot-like. "Anxiety attack countdown."

At that moment, Dara and Veronica both began to squeal. "Omigod, the boys are here!" I turned to look and noticed a group of about five very cute Manhattan boys walking through the door, not breaking their swagger or their formation. I recognized one of them as Alex Altfest—the prince of New York City, according to a lot of my old friends. He had the whole tall, dark, and handsome thing going on, and he managed to be impeccably dressed in a forest green Fendi sweater without looking like he cared too much about his clothes. The others were basically attractive clones of him. They must be the A-list at Dalton this year.

Looking at them, even just from afar, made me feel really out of touch with this world.

Dara, Veronica, and Olivia were trying to play it cool, but they quickly started arguing about who should approach the boys first.

"I did it *last* time when we saw him at Papaya King," Dara whispered insistently.

Behind me, I could feel SBB retreating ever further into panic mode. It was crazy what a group of guys could do to a room. But my immediate concern was Sara-Beth. I turned to her and grabbed her hand. "You okay?" I asked. "We can head out if you want."

"Too dangerous," she said in a voice I didn't recognize. It was as if she had turned into an android. "Follow me."

She tugged my hand and pulled us both around a corner. There, down an aisle and to the right, in a whole different room of the store, was a giant steamer trunk. I stared at it. It was easily the biggest piece of luggage I'd ever seen in my life—quite possibly bigger than a MINI Cooper. Before I knew it, SBB tugged me inside, and the trunk closed around us with a soft click. There I was, huddled in a piece of luggage next to SBB, trying to help her control her breathing.

"Meditate at the third eye point," I told her. "That always helps."

"*Shhh,*" she said. "Don't leave."

"Sara-Beth, I don't really have anywhere to go." The walls of the trunk pressed up against us, and only a glimmer of light came through the hinges.

"Let's just *be* for a few minutes. I think it will help, okay?"

"Okay." But it was clearly not okay, since SBB was gripping my forearms so hard that I could feel her nails digging into my skin.

Once SBB's breathing had quieted, I was able to hear sounds from the outside. "Oh Alex, guess who you just missed?" Olivia said. "Flan Flood! She was just here. I don't know where she went. She looked amazing, didn't she? Maybe *I* should have gone to Stuyvesant."

This made the other girls laugh—and I almost didn't hear Alex say, "Well, Flan was always a hottie."

My eyes grew wide and even SBB put her panic attack aside for a minute to nudge me and giggle. Now we *definitely* couldn't come out of the steamer trunk until everyone was gone.

"I have a credit card here for *Flan Flood*," a French-accented voice rang out. *Crap.* It was the snotty saleswoman, blowing our cover. The way she called my name out made it sound like a dead fish falling to the floor with a *thump*.

"What do we do?" I asked SBB.

Sara-Beth put back on the Texas drawl and said loudly through the trunk, "Um, ma'am, we were fixin' to look at this steamer trunk, and we happened to get ourselves stuck."

There were muffled giggles from the other side, and I heard one of the girls whisper, "Who knows? She's from *Texas*," before the saleswoman came over with the key. I was ready to breathe in the sweet air of freedom and deal with the embarrassment of falling out of a steamer trunk in front of a high-profile audience, but SBB can never do anything the normal way. She had other plans.

The steamer trunk opened a crack and we saw the dour face of the saleswoman and a glimpse of my friends standing just behind her. But before the door opened all the way, SBB grabbed the saleswoman by the name tag on her lapel and pulled her partway into the trunk.

"Angie," she said in an urgent voice. "Look, I'm sorry about this, but I'm a movie star." She flicked up her sunglasses briefly to show her face. "See? Sara-Beth Benny. I don't usually do this, but I need to ask you a favor."

Angie let out that weird, excited exhale of someone really into meeting famous people.

Sara-Beth continued talking. "My ESP tells me there's a load of paparazzi waiting outside this door, and I *know* you don't want them in your store. They break things, trample on nice luggage, and blind customers with their awful camera flashes. It's bad for business."

Angie's forehead wrinkled, and we watched her glance out the door.

"What can I do to help?" Angie asked.

"What you have to do is this," SBB hissed. "Lock up this little steamer trunk—I love it, by the way, I'll take two—and crate my friend and me out to a loading van in the back. Don't forget Flan's little duffel out there, too. Your driver will take us home and we'll avoid any ugly situations with the press. Okay?"

"I'm afraid that's not possible," Angie said, biting her lip and looking back toward the cash register. I could see my old friends staring at us, whispering curiously.

"Look, *Ange*, I'm on strict doctor's orders to indulge my panic attacks, and this is the way I choose to indulge this one. If it's going to cost me, it's going to cost me. I'm happy to write you a check."

Angie raised her precisely tweezed eyebrows at us.

"Would you like an autographed copy of the *I Do Till Timbuktu* DVD?" SBB was flailing. "You look like a Patrick Dempsey fan; I can get him to stop into the store. I'll take *three* steamer trunks if you want. Just lock us back up in this trunk and get us home. *Capisce*?"

"Fine," she sighed. "I'll . . . see what I can do. But I want that DVD."

When the doors closed around us again, even I felt safer.

"How did you do that?" I asked her.

"You just have to know what you want, Flan. Secret of life," she said in her last bit of Texas drawl. Then she sighed and turned serious. "I'm so glad you were here, Flanny. I don't know what I'd have done without you. Promise me we'll always be close to each other's hearts."

SBB put her arms around me, and I leaned into her. Yes, she's totally insane, but she's also my best friend. Soon I felt the lift of a dolly carting our trunk to the back of the store.

"Of course I promise," I said. "We're steamer sisters now. And that's a bond that lasts forever."

"*Steamer sisters*! Oh my God, Flan, I love that!" SBB hammered on the side of the trunk with her little fist, and I swear I could see her eyes glowing in the darkness. I was a little scared, sure, but in a good way.

Chapter 6

*I*t was Monday morning, and things were looking up.

After being carted back like a zoo animal to SBB's pad by one very grumpy UPS driver yesterday afternoon, I thought I might be permanently scarred. Luckily, from my cushy seat today on our all-business class flight to Nevis, the claustrophobic memory of the steamer trunk debacle was fading fast.

I stretched out my legs and reclined my leather seat back. I was next to the window with Judith beside me. Meredith was across the aisle. As we waited at the gate for the plane to finish boarding, a flight attendant came by with hot hand towels, toasty spiced nuts, and virgin Bloody Marys.

"Anybody want an Airborne?" Judith said, opening her backpack to reveal a pharmacy's worth of drugs.

Meredith stuck an eye out of her aromatherapy eye

62

mask and said, "You're not supposed to mix pills with Bloody Marys."

"Hello—virgin means no vodka. It's totally fine," Judith said, popping two of the pills. "Airplanes are basically breeding grounds for infectious diseases."

She wiggled the white container at me.

"No thanks," I said. "I'm good."

"Don't blame me when you develop strep throat," she said, and began rooting through the seat pocket in front of her. "Ugh, does anyone's magazine *not* have the crossword puzzle filled in already?"

It was funny the way people's quirks seemed to magnify while traveling. We hadn't even taken off yet, and already I was thinking it might be a long five-hour flight.

I sat up straight in my seat to scope out what my parents and Feb were up to a few rows ahead. Feb was already passed out—that girl can fall asleep anywhere. She had opened the door literally right as we were getting into the car to drive to the airport, and she didn't even pack—she just got into the car with us and fell asleep. My mom was on her second mimosa, and she was nuzzling her nose into my dad's. *Ew.* I slouched back down in my seat.

"Hey, Meredith," I called across the aisle. "Got any more of those eye masks?"

"Shhh," she returned from under her mask, "beauty rest in progress."

Just then, the flight attendant reappeared with a wooden box, which she opened in front of us. "Did someone say eye mask?" she asked.

Inside the box was an assortment of jewel-colored satin eye masks that made Meredith's look like it was a blue light special from Kmart. Judith and I each thanked the flight attendant and took one.

Just then Mer tossed off her eye mask and turned to us. "I changed my mind. I'm way too excited to sleep," she said. "I can't believe a week ago I thought I'd be making green bean casserole with Grandma on Thanksgiving, and now here we are, en route to Paradise. What do you guys want to do first? I was reading a book about Nevis, and it said there are some really good cave explorations you can go on."

"Are you going to be in Vacation Dictator Mode all week?" Judith asked Meredith. She was wearing an eye mask on her head like Rambo and had pulled out the trig flash cards I'd forgotten to tell her to leave at home. By now she was arranging them by their color-coded tabs.

Meredith stuck her tongue out and said, "Are you going to study all week?"

"I think there might be some sort of bonfire on the beach tonight," I said, trying to lighten the mood.

"*Cool*," Meredith said.

"So, what kinds of people are going to be there?" Judith asked me.

As if on cue, a line of girls who looked our age boarded the plane and sauntered down the aisle right past us. Each of them wore a differently colored, wool woven poncho with a white tank top underneath. They all carried some variation of a Louis Vuitton travel bag. As they walked down the aisle, they looked painfully intimidating, like a skinny and perfectly blown out poncho force field.

"Who are *they*?" Judith asked me, as if I was expected to know everyone on the plane.

I shrugged my shoulders and tried to look disinterested. The truth was, the girls *did* look familiar. But there's a certain Manhattan private school girl look, so maybe I knew them, or maybe I just knew their type. There was something about the way they had walked onto the plane that unsettled me. If I had gone to Thoney, I probably would have known them, and the fact that I didn't made me feel on the outside of a social scene I used to be totally plugged in to.

"Are they part of our group, Flan?" Meredith asked.

"I don't know," I said, a tad more forcefully than I meant to. "I mean," I softened my voice, "there's a whole big group coming. I'm sure we'll meet everyone tonight at the party."

Meredith and Judith were both looking at me wide-eyed, like lost puppies at the pound. I didn't want them to stress about tonight, even though seeing those other girls made me a little nervous, too. It would be in my best interest to play happy hostess to my friends and make them feel totally comfortable.

"Don't worry, you guys, the trip is going to be amazing, I promise. We have a sweet bungalow all to ourselves, and once we get there, our biggest concerns will be which flip-flops match our bathing suits best."

Both of them nodded and looked so relieved that I wondered how much stock they put into what I said. Judith refocused on her cards, and Meredith even flipped through her in-flight magazine to find an empty crossword puzzle for Judith. The captain came on and announced that we were almost ready to taxi out and that they'd be closing the boarding gate in a minute.

Just then, I looked up to see a tall figure saunter onto the plane with a canvas bag slung over his shoulder.

"*Sheesh*," Judith said, glancing up. "You'd think if

you were *this* late for a flight, you'd be in a little bit more of a rush. That guy looks like he has all the time in the world. Wait—isn't that—"

"Patch," I said, laughing. Of course my brother would be fashionably late to the flight and not even get the least bit riled up about it.

"Hey, kiddo," he said, reaching out to tug my ponytail as he walked past us toward his seat. "You girls ready for some fun?"

"I didn't know you were on our flight," I said. "Mom said you'd probably just meet us at the bunga-lows."

"Eh," Patch said, giving me a lopsided grin. "I was in the neighborhood." He winked and made his way back to his seat. I could hear some kids behind us call-ing out to him as he crossed the plane. Maybe I knew more people on this plane than I thought I did. My stomach did a little tap dance at that thought, but I wasn't sure if it was in relief or in dread.

A few minutes later, we were in the air. As we took off, we looped around the city and had a great view of the perfectly clear morning down below. Meredith, Judith, and I huddled over my window and tried to point out our apartments, our school, and the spot where we'd had a picnic in Washington Square Park last week, when I'd convinced the girls that it was too nice a November day to be stuck inside.

"I still can't believe you got Judith to skip class," Meredith said, nudging J in the ribs.

"It was so great," I said, as the park got smaller and smaller through the window. "Except remember when that little Chihuahua started terrorizing us?"

"I know," Judith agreed. "I haven't been so scared since that time Noodles jumped on my back at Flan's house, and I nearly fell down the stairs."

"You kind of *did* fall down the stairs," Mer said with a giggle.

"We should do stuff like that picnic break from school more often," I said, turning around to face my friends. "Sometimes I just need an escape from that place."

"What place?" Judith asked, tilting her head. "You mean Stuy?"

"Um . . ." I had said the words before I'd really thought about them, but surely my friends thought high school could be a little suffocating too?

"I know exactly what you mean," Meredith said, coming to my rescue. "I mean, Stuy's a really good school, but sometimes the art program just isn't challenging enough. I should probably be at LaGuardia or some art school in Vermont to really, you know, hone my craft. But you know how my grandma feels about college applications. . . ."

"But Flan doesn't want to go to art school," Judith said. "I thought you loved the classes at Stuy? What is it you need an escape from?"

What would I say if I could be totally honest with her right now? That I sort of missed being in a place like Miss Mallard's where I could recognize everyone and feel recognized by everyone on campus? That last week, when some junior guy spilled his chocolate milk on my bag, he sneered, "Sorry, *Princess*," and all of his friends started laughing? That I often wondered what my old friends were doing in their classes at Thoney?

These were the things that were running through my head, but I knew, looking at my friends waiting on the edges of their cushy leather seats for my answer, that these weren't the kinds of things that Meredith and Judith would get.

"I just think the classes are pretty tough. I'm totally stressing over finals," I said at last.

Again, I saw relief cross their faces. "Yeah, me too," they both agreed.

"But," Meredith said, holding up a finger. "I have another brilliant vacation proposition. I say for one whole week, we're not going to think about that! This should be a no-study week to rejuvenate us for next week when we have to hit the books again. No talking about grades, no ragging on unfair teachers, no mentions of what we have to do before we get back to class on Monday. What happens at Stuy needs to stay at Stuy this week."

"Deal," I said.

"Speak for yourselves," Judith said, waving her note cards menacingly in our faces. "I, for one, plan to ace all my finals."

Luckily, before I could start to feel anxious about my own finals, our in-flight movie clicked on—which happened to be SBB's recent hit, *I Do Till Timbuktu.* We laughed at SBB's hopelessly befuddled romantic missteps as we munched on grapes and chicken caprese salad and cranberry juice spritzers. And before we knew it, the plane touched down in Paradise.

The three of us hurried off the plane so we could grab our bags and start vacationing. Standing at the baggage carousel, everyone around us looked visibly more relaxed than they had in New York. It was a pretty ritzy crowd, so it was funny to see all these uptight New Yorkers suddenly sporting wide-brimmed straw hats and Prada beach shorts. Patch had his arm looped around a couple of waifish girls I'd never seen before. Even the airport itself felt tropical, with palm trees lining the baggage carousel and a warm sea breeze blowing in through the sliding doors. Catching a glimpse of some more exotic plants and tons of white sand outside, I started thinking that Meredith was right. It *would* be easy to forget about high school until Monday. I was with my two best buds and there wasn't a cloud in the sky.

"Okay, time for a kickoff round," Meredith said, as we waited for the bags to start coming out. "*Would You Rather?*" She slyly pointed a finger first at a bleached-blond all-American-looking guy who'd been on our plane, then at one of the very tan, very buff luggage attendants.

"Hmm," I said, smiling. "I might go with the local hottie."

Judith shook her head. "Not me. Blondie all the way."

"Well the nice thing is," Meredith said, as the baggage carousel started to move, "at least you won't have to fight over them!"

The first bag I spotted sliding down the claim belt was my new duffel, followed by M&J's luggage.

"Hey, this is a good sign," I said.

"Totally. It's like they knew we need to be on the beach ASAP," Meredith agreed.

We lugged our suitcases toward the line of Range

Rovers that were waiting outside to take us to our bungalow.

I was just about to hand my new duffel over to a very burly driver when something made me freeze mid-step.

"Flan!" Judith said, nearly crashing into me with her suitcase.

"Are you okay?" Meredith asked, putting her hand on my arm.

Suddenly, I was very much *not* okay, but I couldn't find the words to tell my friends. What I saw before me was a disaster.

In that one instant, I felt every fantasy I'd had about our paradise vacation slip through my fingers like white Caribbean sand.

Chapter 7

What was Kennedy Pearson doing here?

In a flash, I was ripped away from the tropical island of Nevis and stuck back in the one place I'd banished to the recesses of my memory: the agonizing seventh grade. The scene of my great blowout with the enemy. The one moment that had probably shaped my teenage destiny more than any other. Anjelica Dawson's end of the year party.

The deal was this.

Growing up, I'd always had a lot of friends. I would share my pink feather pencil set with anyone in class, I knew how to read tarot cards before most of my friends even knew what they were, and I could hit a softball out of the park because Patch taught me how.

Around the sixth grade, when being "popular" became the singular focus of most of the girls at my school, I never had to try that hard. At the time, I didn't think too much about it—I was just being myself. But looking back, I think some of what made life easy for me had to do with Patch and Feb's influence. I guess from an early age, I'd been exposed to things like movie premieres, posh Hamptons pads, and hard-core partying. And even though I wasn't doing any of the actual drinking or red velvet rope line cutting, according to a lot of the girls at school, I was considered popular by my proximity to cool things. And so, rather than telling girls that they were thinking I was cool for all the wrong reasons, I kind of just didn't deal with it.

So girls came up to me in the locker room for kissing advice before I'd even had a boyfriend of my own. People I barely hung out with would ask for my opinion about the length and cut of their jeans. I got invited to the birthday party of every single kid in the sixth grade.

And wherever I went, so did my best friend Camille. Ever since the second grade, when we realized that we were both left-handed *and* that we both dotted our I's in exactly the same way (with a diamond instead of the typical and frequently overused heart), Camille and I did everything together. And until the end of seventh grade, I thought it would be like that forever.

Then Kennedy Pearson moved to town.

Sure, she was beautiful. And confident. And her clothes were different from ours—cooler in a sense—because she'd just moved from Harvard Westlake in L.A., where no one cared whether they wore a black bra with a white tank top—and where life in general, according to Kennedy, was just so much more chill. Being *chill* was a big thing with Kennedy.

Right away, we inducted her into our clique. Camille and I volunteered to show her the ropes because the kids at Miss Mallard's followed a pretty strict protocol. But I realized soon enough that Kennedy was more interested in showing us *her* ropes than she was in learning ours. For six months, all I heard about was L.A.

In L.A., we only eat with chopsticks.

In L.A., everyone is so over emo.

People are still wearing Uggs here? Really? That never caught on in L.A. with the truly cool people—just the wannabe movie stars.

And one day, I couldn't help it. I just snapped.

"Kennedy, that's because it's eighty degrees in L.A every day. It's negative three in New York, where you live now, if you hadn't noticed."

We were sitting in the cafeteria eating our salads—with chopsticks—and suddenly things got very quiet.

"Whoa, check out the tight-ass," Kennedy said, laughing her throaty laugh, which I realized I was beginning to hate.

From then on, things between us were a little tense. I stopped inviting her everywhere I went and, even though I hated to do it, there were a few times when I even asked Camille to lie to Kennedy when I invited her to go to some new store opening or impossible-to-get-into café. I still remember the weekend of the Spring Break Hamptons Club Crawl and the after-party Patch threw at our Hamptons house when I was in seventh grade. I'd invited Camille out for the weekend, and we'd spent the evening embarrassing ourselves on my karaoke machine. Around midnight, when Patch and his friends trooped home from the Club Crawl and started a bonfire on the beach behind our house, Camille and I sneaked downstairs to get some sodas (read: spy on all the action outside).

Looking out our kitchen windows, I'd caught a glimpse of a frightening sight.

Kennedy was on *my* pier dancing with *my* brother, wearing nothing but a bikini top, a grass skirt, and Uggs!

By the end of school, it was basically a cold war between us. The more I tried not to get involved with

Kennedy, the more she managed to get under my skin. In fact, I almost didn't go to Anjelica's annual end-of-the-year-bash, but then I realized I wasn't going to let one person stop me from having a good time.

I wore a Lacoste sleeveless dress and my thickest skin and vowed to have as much fun as I had had every year up to then.

But all night, I felt on edge. I didn't want to bob for apples like everyone else. The hayride was making me sneeze. I'd forgotten to bring my iPod, so I was the only one who couldn't spotlight DJ when my turn came. And when Kennedy proposed that everyone gather round for a game of spin the bottle, I could feel my whole body tense up. There was no way I was going to have my first kiss take place in public under the direction of Kennedy Pearson.

I tried to convince Camille to ditch the party for a little while and go for a walk down by the beach, but her brand-new crush, Xander Ross, was hanging out, and I could tell Camille was dying to have the bottle point at him when she spun it.

"Come on," I pleaded. "Just grab Xander and see if he wants to go to the beach with us. I bet all the guys think spin-the-bottle is totally lame. You'd actually be able to talk to him for a change if it were just a few of us hanging out."

"Yeah right, Flan," Camille giggled, turning beet-red. "That'd be like asking him out on a *date*. I could never. Let's just stay here and play."

When she saw the negative look on my face, she pulled out the heavy artillery.

"Come on," she said. "Xander's friend . . . that tall guy . . . Alex Altfest will be there. Admit you think he's so cute—you guys would have the best-looking babies. What if you got to kiss him?"

I didn't realize Camille was dragging me by the hand into the living room where the game was about to begin, but as we came through the sliding door, I found myself saying, too loudly, "But I don't want to kiss *anyone* today. Not like this."

Just then, I noticed that Kennedy was standing two feet in front of us. She had one arm around Alex Altfest and moved to put the other one around Camille. As soon as she did that, I felt a draft of cold air wash between Camille and me. In that moment, I knew I really had lost her forever. She'd been sucked in like a magnet to Team Kennedy.

And then came Kennedy's nasally whispered words, which have been burned in my memory ever since:

"Too bad Flan can't ever just mellow out and be chill like Patch and Feb."

A rush of comebacks ran through my head: *You don't know anything about my brother and sister, who are a million times cooler than you!*

Is being a total backstabbing liar considered chill in L.A.?

Even, *Hey everybody, is Kennedy so laid back that she doesn't even realize she needs the next size up in those Citizens jeans?*

Any of those would have been perfectly acceptable . . . if not a little bit out of character and borderline bitchy. But what came out of my mouth was the lamest, most embarrassing line of all.

In a choked, hoarse shout that made me sound like a boy going through puberty, I shouted, *"I can, too!"*

With those three stupid words ringing in my ears, I fled the party in tears. I could hear the room erupt into laugher behind me, and I was sure I was the laughingstock of the entire evening. I spent the worst summer ever in hiding. Camille left a few messages on my phone, but I was too embarrassed to return her calls. Over the course of that summer, I started to worry that Kennedy had been right about me. Maybe I *couldn't* hang. Maybe I *wasn't* chill.

Eighth grade was no picnic. Hardly any of my old friends called me anymore. Even the girls who hadn't been invited to Anjelica's party seemed to have heard about my meltdown. Some steered clear of me as if I had a contagious disease. At first, Camille would wave at me tentatively from the table by the window where we always used to sit, but eventually, she stopped making the effort.

Finally, Patch and Feb came to my rescue, because they couldn't stand to see me commit social suicide weekend after weekend. I started hanging out with them more and more, and soon enough, I'd virtually disappeared from the scene at school. I started dating Jonathan, which was a blast on nights and weekends, but I still had to try to hold my head high at school. The truth was, a lot of the time, I was feeling pretty pathetic.

That spring, I realized I had spent almost a year being mostly miserable. I knew I needed to look for a way to snap myself out of this funk. I needed a fresh start, a clean slate, and some new friends. I needed a new school.

So while my old friends were island-hopping together during Spring Break, I went textbook hopping solo. And it paid off. By May, I got my test scores back from the public high school entrance exam, along with a letter congratulating me on my acceptance to Stuy, hands down the best public high school in Manhattan.

The hardest part about it was selling public school to my parents, who were all about private school. My dad insisted that it was the only place where I could get a real education, and my mom thought it was very important that I keep up with all the families that were connected to ours. But after I made a few of my best pouting faces at opportune moments (while my dad was shaving, while my mom was color-coding her jewelry), they caved. We agreed on a trial period at Stuyvesant.

All of that seemed like eons ago. When I'd walked across the stage at our eighth-grade graduation, I'd made a vow to try and avoid ever seeing Kennedy Pearson again. Nearly a full year had passed since I'd made that promise, and I thought I'd been doing pretty well with my clean high school slate.

But now, standing twenty feet away from her, I felt a flood of insecurities that seemed *so* not me anymore. Why was her hair so voluptuous and shiny? Oh no, she was *not* carrying the same Bric's duffle in navy blue! And how did she already have a clan of followers huddled around her? I scanned their faces to see if Camille was there, but I didn't see her in the crowd. I didn't know if that was a good thing or a bad thing. I was reeling. I needed to sit down.

I reached out in front of me, grabbed Judith's and Meredith's arms, and steadied myself.

"Omigod, Flan, what is it?" Meredith asked. "I've never seen you like this. You're scaring me."

"Tell us what we can do to help," Judith said. "I *knew* I should have made you take an Airborne."

I struggled for words. "I . . . I . . ."

And then I saw Kennedy turn to look at me, and it was like a heat wave and a burst of terrible bright light had hit me at once. *"I can, too!"* Kennedy's mocking voice came booming across the parking lot.

Everyone in the crowd around her looked over at me and burst into one giant laugh. And my heart broke all over again. Tears stung my eyes, and I couldn't bear to even look at Meredith or Judith—who were both totally innocent and clueless. So much for our paradise vacation.

Where was that giant steamer trunk when *I* needed something to crawl into and hide?

Chapter 8

The next thing I knew, someone was fastening a middle seatbelt around me and someone else was tilting my head back and positioning a bottle of water to my lips.

"Cold, *so cold*," I whispered. I was in the back of one of the Range Rovers, and my friends were on either side of me.

"Here," Judith said. "Drink."

"Ladies," our driver said as he started the car. "You'll be staying in Bungalow Eight."

A blur of palm tree fronds began whizzing past our windows.

"Ooh," Meredith said. "Just like the club. How lucky! Flan, isn't that lucky?"

"Mmm," I think I said out loud.

I caught sight of a billboard for cave diving, one for parasailing, and one showing a huge open-air deck on a gorgeous cliff overlooking the water. I couldn't see the beach yet, but I could smell it. On some level, I knew we were on the way to the bungalow that we'd call home for the next week. But all I could focus on was the extreme embarrassment of the last five minutes and the side order of a very strong and sudden case of nausea that I was dealing with.

"Sooner or later, she's going to have to speak," I heard Judith say over my head to Meredith.

"Do you think one of those guys was her ex-boyfriend?" Meredith whispered back.

"Worse," I managed to moan.

"Flan, you're alive!" Meredith said. "Wait—worse than an ex-boyfriend? What do you mean?"

"Ex-girlfriend," I said, taking the water bottle from Judith and resting it against my forehead.

Judith's eyes looked like they were about to bug out of her head. "You never told us you—"

"No, no," I said. "Not *that* kind of ex-girlfriend. It was Kennedy Pearson. A girl I used to be friends with at my old school. That is, before she turned into my nemesis."

"Oh," Judith said. "You're right, that *is* worse." She looked over at Meredith. "Remember Jana Walsh?"

Meredith grimaced. "You say that as if I could forget Jana Walsh."

Judith turned back to me. "Jana Walsh was the other point in our triangle way back in the sixth grade. The three of us were best friends all through elementary school."

"You've never mentioned anyone named Jana Walsh before," I said.

The girls nodded gravely.

"There's a reason for that. Remember the Tony Incident?"

"Of course," I said. Tony was a hot guy from M&J's old school. He was the reason we enacted the No Adam Rule in the first place, because the girls had (supposedly) learned their lesson after both lusting after the same guy once before—with disastrous results.

"Well," Judith said, "after Meredith and I decided that our friendship was more important than some lame video-game-playing, prepubescent—"

"You mean after we totally freaked him out by waging a screaming fight over him in front of an audience?" Meredith interrupted with a laugh. "Well, the point is, Flan, that after that—"

"Our *best friend,* Jana Walsh, stepped in and stole him right out from under us," Judith finished. Then, an embarrassed look crossed her face. She froze and there was an awkward silence before she said, "Oh, but she was totally bitchy about it and neither of us ever got over it. She wasn't half as mature and honest with us as you've been about Adam. Anyway, what I mean is, Meredith and I totally know what it's like to have an ex-best friend who you never wanted to see again. Right, Mer?"

Meredith nodded and quickly changed the subject. "What'd this Kennedy girl do, anyway? Please don't tell me she tried to steal your boyfriend."

"Worse," I said, feeling like a broken record. "She *succeeded* in stealing my *best* friend."

The 'diths nodded again. They put their arms around my shoulders.

"You're right," Judith said. "That is much, much worse."

"So what are we going to do about it?" Meredith asked.

It was hard to feel so shaken up and numb while looking out the windows as we drove. The stereo was playing Bob Marley on low, and the windows were rolled down all the way so that the most fabulous breeze tossed our hair around. Everything outside was just so lush and green and incredibly, incredibly beautiful that I couldn't help but be warm again.

"Nothing," I said, somehow managing to put on a braver face than I felt. "We're not going to let her bother us. We're going to go through with all the things we said we'd do this week. We're going to— whoa!"

We had just turned into a circular driveway that opened up on a massive two-story white stucco house with a faux thatched roof and a long wooden staircase down to the beach. This was no quaint little bunga- low. This was the lap of luxury.

"'Whoa' is right," Meredith said. "This can't be for us?"

"Ladies," the driver said, stopping the car. "This is Bungalow Eight." He opened our car doors and began to carry our suitcases into the house.

Meredith and Judith stood there, stunned for a minute, and then all three of us dashed for the door.

Inside, our pad was decked out in super elegant island décor. There were three bedrooms—each with an ocean view. The upstairs living room had a giant wraparound deck with a hot tub and a row of ham- mocks, each shaded by different brightly colored, blossoming hibiscus trees.

We claimed our rooms and began roaming around the property, calling out to one another about each fantastic discovery we made.

"The fridge is stocked with tropical fruit salad and Honest Tea!" Meredith gushed.

"And there's snorkeling gear in the pool shack!" Judith shouted.

"Hey, you guys," I called. "Come check this out."

On the kitchen table, I'd found a folder that must have been left for us by one of the members of the Zumbergs' extensive vacation staff. Inside were a map of the island and a listing of each bungalow's phone number. My parents—and in fact all of the adults—were staying in a line of hilltop cottages on the beach cove right up from us. That was at least two miles away, so I knew that the parties on our beach would be pretty off the hook.

There was also a detailed social schedule of events for the entire week. It was broken down into different activities for the kids and for the adults—and our schedule included a bonfire party down on the beach that night.

"Jackpot!" Meredith said. "What are you guys going to wear?"

Judith took the schedule from my hands. "Monday night is the bonfire. Tuesday night is a beach-side barbecue. There's an afternoon snorkeling expedition. Today there's an Island Adventure Scavenger Hunt. Um, is this a vacation or a military schedule? It's like every minute is already planned out." She flipped her hair anxiously. "You said it was going to be relaxing, Flan. I'm already stressing. When will I have time to study?"

"Judith, we don't have to go to everything," I said. "We can pick and choose whatever we want. This schedule's just here to give us options. Don't worry—there'll be plenty of free time. Usually people go to things the first night in order to make friends, and then make their own plans after that."

"Personally," Meredith said, taking a sip of pomegranate Honest Tea, "I want to do everything." She pointed at the first group activity this afternoon. "I mean, how many times in your life have you had the opportunity to go on an Island Adventure Scavenger Hunt?"

"I know I'm only going to have this set of finals *once,* so I have to set aside a ton of time to study like crazy," Judith said.

"I think the secret is pacing ourselves," I said. "Pick and choose what we want, skip what we don't. That's the great thing about vacation—we can do whatever we feel like doing."

I was glad that Meredith seemed so into it all. She dashed off to change into her bathing suit for the scavenger hunt, while Judith hauled out her seven hundred-page math book. I felt that a more leisurely pace was in order, so I wandered out to the deck and climbed into one of the hammocks in the shade.

"Why don't we reconvene here at seven o'clock to get ready for the bonfire tonight?" Meredith called on her way out the door.

I gave her the thumbs-up and leaned back in the hammock, listening to how different the sounds of the island were from the sounds of New York. It was so relaxing out here, so peaceful. I couldn't help but close my eyes. . . .

I was walking down an unfamiliar hallway, but I seemed to know not only exactly where I was going, but also every single person I passed.

"Hey, Flan—love your outfit! Is that a new boatneck top? You should always wear those!"

"Flan, you have to promise you'll run for class president this year. You're the only one who can lead our grade."

"Flan, my cousin, Zac Efron, is coming into town on Friday, and I swore to him that you'd come out to dinner with us. Is there any chance you're free?"

Of course, I suddenly realized. I was at Thoney, starting classes at the beginning of second semester. Everything felt so easy here, so natural. I was practically floating down the hallway. I smiled at everyone, waved at everyone.

Flan for President? Why not?

Of course I'm free to hang with you and Cousin Zac.

I got to my locker, which didn't even have a combination—it just sprang open when I stopped in front of it. How wonderful! I could never remember my combination at Stuy. I was about to take out my books for my afternoon classes, when I made the mistake of glancing in the mirror of my LockerMate.

Looking back at me was not my reflection at all. It was the face of Kennedy Pearson.

"You think you can rule the school so easily, Flan?" Her nasty voice practically spat at me. "Well, guess what? You're wrong! Remember, I can, too!"

I gasped in horror and slammed the locker shut.

"Hey, Sleeping Beauty, wake up and check this out."

I shot up in the hammock. My heart was racing. I rubbed my eyes and noticed Meredith in the hammock next to mine. Something hard landed on my stomach, and when I reached for it, my fingers found a necklace.

It was made of abalone shells and the weird wooden beads that Meredith had shown us last week at Alice's Tea Cup. But somehow, the weird wooden beads didn't look so weird anymore. The necklace was slightly longer than a choker and was actually kind of great.

"You made this?" I said, still a little out of it from my intense dream.

Meredith grinned and nodded. "I found the abalone shells in the scavenger hunt. And I met some of the absolute greatest people. I can't wait to introduce you tonight. Everyone's going to this bonfire. Anyway, when I came home, I just knew the shells would look great with my new beads. Check out how great Judith's looks."

Judith stepped forward and modeled the necklace she was wearing. It did look really cool. But I was still stuck on what Meredith had said about the scavenger hunt. Exactly which absolute greatest people had she met?

"I don't know if it's the necklace that suits you so well," Meredith said to Judith, "or if you just look so much better without that trig book weighing you down."

"Ha-ha, shut up," Judith said. "Let's put Flan's necklace on her."

I stood up and let the girls fasten the necklace. When I looked at it in the mirror, all I could think of was how grateful I was to be awake, and that it was my own reflection I saw before me—not Kennedy Pearson's.

Chapter 9

An hour later, we were ready to party. Judith was wearing a jean skirt and a bright orange graphic T-shirt that said MEET ME IN RIO. Mer had on a long red sarong that she'd wrapped herself in like an origami doll. And I was wearing a short cream-colored tunic dress with a purple hibiscus flower in my hair. All three of us were sporting Meredith's new necklaces, and there were no sensible shoes or boat-neck tops or mismatched patterns to be found.

We made our way toward the circle of tiki torches that outlined the bonfire below. I could hear the buzz of the party competing with the sound of the waves washing up on the shore. The sun was setting, and a few stars were already popping out. I was definitely in the mood for some fun, but I was still a little bit nervous about whom we'd find when we got there.

"Oh my God," Meredith breathed as we got close

enough to see what people were wearing. "Everyone's so glamorous. From a purely artistic perspective, this is *amazing*."

She was right. It was definitely a posh-looking crew. The poncho girls had shed their cover-ups and were making do in Pucci bikini tops and designer cut-offs. A group of kids were trying to have a hula hoop contest, but they kept tripping over their feet and collapsing on top of each other in fits of laughter.

"They're not even doing it right," Judith huffed, flipping her blond hair over her shoulders. She still sounded stressed, and I knew I needed to figure out a way to get her to relax and have some fun. But I was feeling pretty preoccupied myself, scanning the party for Kennedy's dark, wavy hair.

"Um, I think it's because they've had a little bit of the island punch, Judith," I said distractedly.

Judith crossed her arms over her chest, looking slightly put out.

Meredith waved at a few kids as we walked into the thick of the crowd. "Hey, Paul," she said to a boy with white-blond hair. He was the guy Judith had picked during *Would You Rather* at the airport.

"Hi, Rena," Mer said to a superskinny girl with big eyes and a splash of freckles across her nose. "You have to meet my friends, Flan and Judith," she said.

And then, turning to us, she explained, "We bonded on the scavenger hunt today."

"How's it going?" I said.

"Awesome," Paul said, sounding like a total surfer. "How huge is this bonfire?"

"Huge!" Judith agreed, and I was glad to see her smile.

The bonfire was so large that it was impossible to see the other side of it. But we could hear a lot of people laughing over there, and it seemed like that was where the action was, so we kept walking around the circle.

When we reached the other side, I stopped short. It shouldn't have surprised me to see Kennedy Pearson holding court with about fifteen of the most popular-looking kids on the beach, but I still wasn't prepared to find myself right in front of her again so quickly.

"It's so loud here," Judith said, covering her ears. "How much longer do you guys want to stay?"

"Judith," I said, much more sharply than I'm sure I meant to. "We just *got* here! And we're on *vacation*."

Judith blanched but didn't answer me. I must have said it more loudly than I realized because at that moment, a really hot guy brushed past us with four drinks in his hands. He gave me a shocked look, like he couldn't believe anyone would be that bitchy.

Ugh, what was wrong with me? The judgmental hottie was right. I wasn't being myself, and I could tell Judith was pretty hurt.

"Look, Judith, I didn't mean—"

But before I had a chance to apologize, Kennedy Pearson appeared right in front of us like the wicked witch she was.

"Flan Flood, look at you. You've certainly grown *up,* haven't you?" she said.

"Hi, Kennedy." I rocked awkwardly on my heels and pulled on my shell necklace. I hated that she could still unsettle me so much.

She looked Judith up and down.

"Where'd you get your friend?" she said. "The same place you got that outfit? The Barney's co-op sale?"

"Oh, no," a familiar voice said behind me. "Flan can only shop at the Big and Tall stores these days."

I spun around. Oh my God. *Meredith* said that? In front of Kennedy? I couldn't tell if she only meant it as a joke, but it definitely felt like an insult.

"I knew there was something I liked about you, Mer," Kennedy said. "Come over to our side of the fire. I want you to meet some of my friends." She spun on her heel and was gone.

I grabbed Meredith's arm.

"I forgot to tell you," she said, looking sheepish. "I met Kennedy on the scavenger hunt this afternoon. I know you have a beef with her, but I swear, she was so nice to me that I almost forgot about it. It seems like she's grown up a lot since middle school. I promise—she's so cool now. She even told me what good friends you used to be and how bad she feels that you two don't hang out anymore."

I opened my mouth to respond, but I was too stunned to speak. Meredith had just basically insulted me to my face, and now she was BFF with Kennedy? What planet had I woken up on? There was no way I was buying the fact that Kennedy felt badly about what happened between us. If there was one thing I knew for certain, it was that Kennedy could *not* be trusted.

I turned to Judith for support, but she was nowhere to be found. I felt terrible. I turned around to find her and apologize, but Meredith took my hand.

"You're not mad, are you?"

"Meredith, you don't know Kennedy. She's evil."

"I really think she's changed," Meredith said, tucking her hair behind her ears. "She was super sweet today. And her parents own this gallery in Chelsea— you know the one I love on 19th Street that I'm always unsuccessfully trying to drag you to? And did you know that Ava Korner is her godmother? You never told me that! You know she's, like, my favorite artist ever. Kennedy said she'd introduce me."

"Meredith, over here!" It was Kennedy, waving *my* friend over to *her* headquarters. I was having déjà vu.

"Let's go," Meredith said. "Just for a little. If you're having a terrible time in five minutes, we can leave. Just give her another chance, okay?"

But she didn't give me any time to argue. She was already halfway to Kennedy. I had no Judith and no choice but to follow Meredith pathetically, like a lost puppy.

"Hey!" Kennedy said as we sat down in the middle of a crowd of cute guys. "TZ, this is Meredith. And that's her friend, Flan. TZ has been wanting to meet you since I told him all about you this afternoon, Meredith."

TZ was none other than the judgmental hottie whom I'd already embarrassed myself in front of. As I looked at him more closely, I realized that I knew him. I'd met him years before. He was Terrick Zumberg—of the Zumbergs who were behind this whole vacation. He'd been a terror when he was a little kid, when he still went by Terrick, but apparently in the few years since I'd seen him he'd bloomed into a full-fledged hunk.

"Hey," TZ said, giving Meredith a smile and a little head nod. "Love your necklace. This is Bruce," he said, pointing down to a very frisky border collie that was trying to gnaw through a coconut.

And I could tell from the way TZ said those seven little words that he knew exactly how cute he was, that he was well aware that everyone here was hanging out on his family's dime, and that there was no question that he could get any girl at this party.

Normally, I hated that kind of guy, but there was something about TZ that was almost magnetic. And soon I noticed that I wasn't the only one staring at him. A girl I knew from Miss Mallard's, Mattie Hendricks, was practically boring a hole in his head with her eyes.

Mattie had been in my history class a few years ago and would be an eighth grader now. I'd always thought she was super sweet, but a little bit on the dorky side. She'd been wearing the same side ponytail since before it was cool again.

"Hey, Mattie," I said to her.

It took her a second to pry her eyes off of TZ, but when she finally looked at me, her face lit up. "Flan! It's so good to see you. I miss you!"

"Oh," I stammered, surprised by her excited tone. "It's good to see you, too."

"Remember when we did that diorama on the Pilgrims three years ago? That was awesome."

I smiled at her. "Yeah," I said. "That was fun."

"Is that your friend over there talking to Terrick Zumberg?"

I looked over to see who she was talking about, and was surprised to see TZ fingering Meredith's necklace.

"That's my friend Meredith?" It had come out sounding like a question.

"So are they dating or what?"

"No!" I said, a little too quickly. I didn't know why, but there was something about that question that made me almost . . . jealous.

I needed to calm down.

I turned to Mattie. "Listen, I'm going to go grab a drink, okay? It was good to see you."

I waved to Mattie and was going to ask Meredith if she wanted to come with me to get some punch from the cooler on the other side of the fire, but when I got there, Kennedy was monopolizing her.

"Oh my God," she said. "Is that necklace made from the shells we found on the beach? I knew you said you were going to do something with them, but I didn't realize you could make such awesome jewelry."

"Well," Meredith said, clearly glowing, "I had a

feeling they'd go well with these new beads I just ordered, but I had to see them together to make sure."

"Wow," TZ said, brushing his dark hair out of his eyes. "That's rad. Could you make me a necklace? You must be really creative."

Telling Meredith she was creative was like telling me, *Hey, Flan, you're even more laid back than your sister and brother.* It was the compliment she most wanted to hear. And the thing was, it was true. She *was* creative. And normally I'd be psyched that someone was giving my friend such well-deserved props, but tonight, it made me feel weird and possessive.

In so many ways I felt like Meredith had been my discovery. Like she was some submerged sea treasure I'd found on a scuba diving trip and had brought to the surface. It wasn't that I didn't want anyone else to see how great she was, it was just that . . . well . . . what *was* it?

And just when I thought things couldn't get any more confusing, I heard Meredith say coyly (and very uncharacteristically), "Uh uh, it doesn't work that way. I can't just make a necklace on demand for anyone who asks."

"Not even for me?" TZ said, fake pouting. It was

startling how he still looked sort of cute with his lower lip turned down.

Meredith looked to the sky, as if for inspiration. "It's just, I have to feel the *need* to make the necklace."

Too much! I needed some air. Luckily, no one was paying any attention to me, so I was able to steal away from the group and get down to the beach. I just wanted to breathe for a few minutes so I could figure out what was making me feel so unsettled about Meredith.

I collapsed on an empty sand bar and watched the waves foam across the shoreline. It was weird. I was practically witnessing Meredith blossom into cool. It was something I'd wanted to happen for months—but the thing that I hated to admit was . . . I always thought that I'd have more to do with it.

I'd tried to coax Meredith out of her shell a thousand times, but as it turned out, she didn't even need my help. In fact, Meredith didn't need to come out of her shell at all; she just needed to make a necklace out of one. I couldn't understand how she was suddenly a smash success at this party. I mean, she was great and all, but in more of a Stuyvesant-great kind of way.

"Um, excuse me?" I looked up to see that a guy

had approached me. I sat up straight and smiled at him. He was kind of cute.

"Yes?"

"You're, uh, I think you're sitting on my girlfriend's poncho." He pointed at the sand where I noticed I was sitting on a woven navy poncho.

"Oh," I said. "Sorry." I handed it to him so he could return it to whichever poncho girl was his girlfriend.

When he started to walk away, I felt more alone than ever. What was I doing out here pouting by myself? I stood up and took a few deep breaths before following the couple back toward the party. As I walked behind them, I, um, accidentally eavesdropped on their conversation.

"We have to wait till the party dies down," the girl was saying. "Kennedy doesn't want a mass exodus. There's only room for ten of us in the kayaks."

"When do you think that's going to be?" her boyfriend asked. "It's already almost midnight."

She shrugged. "Whenever TZ says the party's over, the party's over. It's always more fun when it's just the late-night crew hanging out anyway."

"Totally. Remember last year with the—"

But I couldn't hear the rest of their story because they both exploded into laughter. It was the kind of laughter that felt so good to do yourself—but felt so bad to hear from the outside.

Or maybe I was just primed to feel sorry for myself. I had never felt so uncool. I'd been so sure that I needed a vacation, but who could call this a relaxing getaway? Definitely not me . . .

$\mathcal{D}$uring my short stint as SBB's landlord this past fall, she used to stumble down the stairs after a night out and bemoan her extreme exhaustion while I was getting ready for school.

"If it sucks this much in the morning," I asked her one morning when the moaning was particularly woeful, "then why don't you party a little less?"

She looked at me like I was a newborn puppy and staggered over to pinch my cheek. "Honey, it hurts so *good.* Everybody loves to say, *Oh, I'm never staying out till sunrise again, la la la.* But really, feeling like crap the next morning is the best reminder that you had yourself a kick-ass time the night before."

I looked at her warily as she buttoned my cardigan in the foyer.

"Someday you'll understand," she said. "But no rush—you're still a kid!" She bopped me on the head, which she had to stand on her tiptoes to do, and sent me off to school.

Fast forward to the present: it was Tuesday, our second morning in Nevis, and the nausea I woke up with was definitely *not* a sign of a good time had the night before. I'd gotten too much sleep, and I still felt sick about pretty much everything going on in my life.

All I wanted was my own bed back at my own house, with a few kisses from Noodles and possibly an order of pancakes from EJ's.

Then again, I was dying to know what had become of Meredith and Judith. I felt uncharacteristically out of the loop. Last night, after I'd overheard Kennedy's plans for the exclusive late-night kayaking expedition, I'd fled the party to avoid being shunned all over again. I locked myself in my room and pumped up the most depressing music playlist on my iPod.

Now it was nine in the morning, and I was feeling guilty about leaving Judith alone for the rest of the night and curious about whether Meredith had made the after-party cut. So I dragged myself out of bed and did an SBB-like stumble downstairs.

The kitchen was empty, save for the navy folder with the jam-packed itinerary reminding me of all the events we were supposed to enjoy this week. Had it only been yesterday when we looked through that folder and got totally pumped about the bonfire? *That* had been a major bust.

I was just about to leaf through the folder to see what I should avoid today—if I didn't want to feel as insignificant as the gunk under Kennedy Pearson's fake nails—when I heard the distinctly metallic sound of a zipper in the next room.

I stuck my head into the living room and saw Judith, fully dressed and struggling to get all her books stuffed back into her suitcase.

"What are you doing?" I asked.

"I'm basting a turkey," she said from her crouched position on the floor. "What does it look like I'm doing? I'm going home."

"You've got to be kidding," I said, feeling for the sofa so I could sit down. I was starting to get a bit dizzy.

She looked at me but said nothing.

"Judith, why?"

"It was a bad idea to come in the first place. Right before finals? Hello, this is, like, *the* worst week to not have access to the library and the Internet."

"I saw an Internet café on the map," I said. I knew I was flailing and that this was a poor way to convince her to stay. Sure, she was a little intense sometimes, but

Judith's snarky sarcasm and constant consideration for her friends was a major part of what was going to make this week so much fun. She couldn't leave!

"It's not just that," she said. "You're . . . *different* on vacation. You made me feel really uncomfortable last night."

"Judith, I feel terrible about the way I acted last night. I know you didn't need me to remind you that we're on vacation—especially not in such a rude way. I was just stressed about things, you know, what with seeing Kennedy again. I didn't mean to take it out on you."

"Don't apologize. It's okay. I'm just getting in the way here."

"That's so not true," I said, shaking my head. "I never meant to make you feel like that, Judith. I just wanted you to relax so you could have some fun."

Yeah right, like I was one to give out advice about having fun.

"That's the point," Judith said. Her voice wobbled a little. "I don't want to relax. This place is just not my scene, and we both know it."

"You're seriously leaving?" I said, hugging a white throw pillow to my chest.

"There's a car picking me up in ten minutes. My parents helped me figure out an earlier flight home."

She surveyed her bags, giving another fruitless tug at her zipper.

"Can I at least help you with your bag?" I said. I stood up and crossed the room toward her.

She held out an arm like a traffic cop. "Don't bother," she said. "I don't need your help."

"What about Meredith? Did you talk to her? What does she think about you leaving?"

"You'll have to ask her yourself," Judith said. "She didn't come home last night."

My face burned. Everything out of her mouth seemed to throw salt on my wounded ego.

You're the reason I'm having a terrible time.

I'd rather bust my suitcase than have you touch it to help me.

Meredith pulled an all-nighter, and you weren't invited.

Perfectly timed to coincide with my aching head and heart, a car horn blared outside.

"That'd be my ride," Judith said. She hauled her half-zipped suitcase up over her shoulder and didn't even look at me as she walked toward the door.

"Judith, wait. You can't just walk out on our vacation."

"Save the breakup speech for Adam," she said. She must have seen the look on my face, because she softened. "Look, let's just let each other mellow out. Call me after finals next week. I'll be able to focus on all this . . . *drama* then."

Before I had a chance to respond, she turned and walked out the door. In a moment, the car had sped away. And just like that, a big piece of my anchor at Stuy had fallen away. Sure, I'd call her after finals . . . but then what? We'd pretend like this never happened? Like we'd never realized that our scenes were pretty much as opposite as you could get? If we couldn't even have a good time here in Paradise, were we wrong about just how good of friends we really were?

As I stood, stunned, on the front porch, Meredith came bolting up the front path. She skidded to a halt when she saw me standing there, as if I were her keeper.

"Oh. Hey," she said, catching her breath.

"Oh, hey."

She was still dressed in her sarong from last night. I would have thought someone doing the walk of shame home would flaunt it a little bit less.

"Judith went home," I said. "To New York."

"Oh no," she said, but the words were completely flat.

"You couldn't care less?" I said.

"I *said* 'oh no.'" Meredith crossed her arms.

"She was having a terrible time."

"That's impossible. It's so amazing here." She frowned. "I don't get it. Why didn't she say something?"

"She did say something," I said. "If you'd been home, you would have heard her." I chose to leave out the part about Judith leaving only because of how badly I'd made her feel last night.

Now Meredith did look like she felt guilty. "Crap. I fell asleep at Kennedy's last night. It was so late when we got home from kayaking and too dark to walk home by myself. TZ offered to walk me home, but . . ." she trailed off. "Hey, I looked for you last night. What'd you end up doing? Did you have an awesome night, too?"

"Something like that," I said.

It was crazy. For so long, I'd been lying to Meredith and Judith, saying that I *didn't* go to a great party that I *did* go to, just so they wouldn't feel like our lives were totally divergent. And now I was lying to her again, saying I *did* do something fabulous just to keep up with her? We couldn't seem to get in sync.

"You must feel like me, then," Meredith said. "I'm practically sleepwalking right now."

Meredith did look exhausted. Her sarong was rumpled and bunched in all the wrong places. She looked like a tablecloth after a long dinner party. Her eyes had bags under them, and her hair desperately needed to be washed.

But somehow, her face was glowing. Her wild time last night had pumped some life into her, and I had to admit, it suited her. She definitely had the hurts-so-good thing going on.

"Yeah," I lied. Again. "I'm probably going to go take a nap, too."

"Oh, I'm not taking a nap," she said. "There's way too much fun stuff going on. Caffeine will have to do for now." She jogged past me and into the kitchen, where I heard her rummaging through the fridge. She came back gulping a can of Starbucks DoubleShot espresso. "Love this stuff. Do you want to shower first, or can I? I think the yacht leaves in an hour."

"What yacht?" I said.

She paused mid-sip. "You're not coming? I figured you were in on it."

"I didn't see a yacht on the itinerary." Even saying those words aloud made me feel like a total geek. Of course this wasn't the type of yacht trip to be on the itinerary. Just like the late-night kayaking hadn't been on the itinerary.

"No, it's . . . oh, it's just this thing Kennedy organized. I'm sure you can come if you want. If you haven't already made plans for yourself."

It was hard to tell which one of us the role reversal shocked more: Meredith or me. Both of us were used to things being the other way around.

Meredith looked deep into her Starbucks can, as if the answer to why things between us were suddenly a little tense was hidden at the bottom of it.

I had nothing to do and no cool friends to even consider meeting up with, but there was no way I was going to play tagalong with Kennedy—even if Meredith did swear she was different now. It'd be better for both of us if I just kept lying through my teeth.

"Yeah, I might hop on a boat to one of the nearby islands for the afternoon," I said, feeling terrible that I was making up all of these plans.

"Well, cool," Meredith said, draining the last of her drink. "We'll have a lot of good stories to swap over dinner tonight."

"Yeah," I said. "I guess we will."

But Meredith was already inside the house, running to claim the first shower so she could make the yacht departure in time.

I flopped down on a chaise lounge on the porch and fought the urge to cry. Instead, I pulled out my cell phone and texted SBB.

SOCIAL SHIPWRECK ON NEVIS. SOS.

Chapter 11

A few hours later, the sun was high in the sky, and I was still down in the dumps. I was lying on the beach, zoning out while watching the fantastically clear blue water. In an attempt to feel cool, I'd even put on my Rachel McHenry bathing suit, but the only people around to see it were an old man and his gold digger wife a few feet down and several older, hairless, Speedo-wearing Italian tourists playing some unusual game of Frisbee that involved a lot of wrestling. I thought I'd recognized the bleach-blond surfer guy, Paul, whom I'd met last night, but when I tapped him on the shoulder and he turned around, it was a guy I'd never seen before.

"Oh," I said. "Sorry."

"Whatever," he said, and turned back around.

Great, now I was even repelling strangers. All I wanted to do was hide under the biggest umbrella I could find in my bungalow's storage closet. Even the fresh air, fine white sand, and blazing sunshine didn't help shake my bad mood.

If I were to send someone a postcard of my vacation, this is what it would look like: me, friendless and alone on the beach, struggling to read *Pride and Prejudice* for my English class, and even feeling a little jealous of the fictional people in the book who were going to fun parties and being courted by all sorts of men.

At least it was peaceful here.

Peaceful, and quiet, and utterly, utterly boring.

Ho hum.

Then, overhead, I heard the droning of a plane. I thought about the lie I'd told Meredith that morning. In reality, my day was pretty much the opposite of the glamorous island-hopping I'd invented.

I hunkered down under my umbrella and stuck my nose a little deeper into my book. But the noise was getting louder, and suddenly, there was a whole lot of wind blowing sand all up in my business. I exited my umbrella cocoon to investigate.

What the . . . ?

A little bullet-gray puddle jumper was landing right in front of me. I shaded my eyes from the wind.

Was it possible I was seeing a mirage?

But the plane really did touch down on the sand, and a pilot really did get out and give me a small wave. I waved back uncertainly.

He disappeared back into the body of the plane for a minute, and when I spotted his trim white uniform again, he was lugging something giant and boxy and incredibly heavy-looking behind him.

Oh. My. Gosh.

Was that what I thought it was?

Then, a cross-looking stewardess appeared and held out a cocktail napkin like it was a script. She cleared her throat and read aloud, *"Drumroll please."*

I laughed and clapped my hands against my thighs. It was a pretty poor drumroll, but there was no one else around to help.

And then, to my delight, the world's best best friend bolted out of the steamer trunk like the world's smallest football player bursting out of the tunnel before the big game.

"Don't you love to travel in style?" SBB asked, taking a bow.

She was sporting giant aviator glasses, an olive-colored fatigue print catsuit, and a red scarf that blew underneath the slowing plane propellers. She looked as if she'd flown the plane herself, circa 1945.

"Sara-Beth, what are you doing here?"

"Duh," she said, throwing her arms around me. "Saving your life."

"Aren't you still shooting a scene today? I didn't even expect to hear back from you."

"Nonsense. What kind of a friend do you think I am? You did say SOS, didn't you?" She grabbed my arm. "Tell me you weren't just being dramatic."

My face fell. I wish I could say I was just being dramatic.

"No," I admitted. "Things here pretty much royally suck."

"Well then, we'll continue with Operation SOS." She snapped her fingers and turned back toward the plane. "Everybody, let's get to work."

"Everybody" turned out to be the very hot pilot and the flight attendant, whom I wouldn't have expected to be so burly and strong underneath her navy uniform. In an instant, the two of them had hauled the steamer trunk up on their shoulders and were walking it across the beach.

"You're staying?" I asked SBB. It would be so fantastic to have her hang with me in Nevis. Everything about this trip would suddenly look a lot brighter.

"Oh, honey, I can't stay. I wish I could. I practically had to pay off the director to let me take an extended lunch break to come see you. I've got to get back in two hours."

"Then what's with the trunk?"

"This is way more than a trunk! It's my happy place. And I want you to have it. You're my friend in need, indeed!"

"Oh," I said, not sure what else to say. "Thanks, SBB . . ."

"Don't thank me till we get inside, and I show you all the amenities. It's going to make you feel *so* much better."

We followed the pilot and his flight attendant back up the beach to my bungalow. I couldn't help but laugh at what an odd team the two of them made. She was barking out orders to him in some language I didn't understand, and he was nodding quietly and straining to get the trunk through my back door.

"Sara-Beth," I said, "where did you dig up this flight crew?"

She rolled her eyes. "How illegitimate do they look? Both of them are stunt doubles on the set. Luke had a pilot's license and a map to Nevis—and a very nice butt in those pants, don't you think? Anyway, he's been following me around for weeks, ever since we started shooting, so I knew he'd do me a favor. And his questionably female counterpart is just along to do some heavy lifting. *So* sketchy, right?"

"Hey, whatever works," I said, putting my arm around her shoulders.

As they released their grip on the steamer trunk in the middle of my living room, I noticed that the pilot did have a pretty nice butt.

Sara-Beth tipped them and asked them to wait out by the plane. They each saluted me as they walked out.

"I hope the trunk brings you as much happiness as it brings to Sara-Beth," the pilot said to me with an Eastern European accent.

"Thank you," I said, trying hard to stifle a laugh. "Thank you both for everything."

When we were alone, SBB entered her combination to unlock the trunk and pried it open. Gone was the chest of drawers lining the right portion of the trunk. If I remembered correctly, they were what had made the thing feel so claustrophobic when the two of us had used it as our hideaway in the Bric's store. In place of the drawers, she'd had some sort of Murphy Bed installed that extended outward at the push of a bright purple button. There was a light switch, a vanity mirror, and even a mini disco ball. It was more like a small house than a piece of luggage.

"Sara-Beth, you could rent this place out in the city."

"Like I said," she grinned. "It's my happy place. Actually, now it's your happy place for a few days."

She motioned for me to take a seat on the foldout bed. Then she reached into a cupboard on the other side of the trunk and produced two surprisingly chilled bottles of Orangina. My legs barely fit on the bed, but I tucked them under me so I wouldn't make SBB self-conscious again about my growth spurt. Luckily, she was keeping herself busy, popping the tops of the Oranginas with a bottle opener that was built into the wall of the trunk. She plopped down beside me on the bed.

"Now, tell me all of your sorrows," she said. "Oh my God. *No! Who* put that there?"

She pointed at the "wall" that the bed had folded out from, where someone had tacked up a headshot of our talk, dark, and handsome pilot.

"Um, probably your not-so-secret flying admirer," I guessed. "It's a pretty good headshot."

"Luke would *never*," she said. "He's much too shy. You know, this is just the sort of immature humor that is so like Jake Riverdale. Have I complained to you enough about our issues on the set? He's just such a *pig*. How did *he* get the combination for my trunk?

I'm going to—" She cut herself off, and for a second, she seemed to collect herself. Her posture straightened, her breath evened. "This trip is about you, Flan. I won't waste another second talking about how much I hate that egotistical . . . whoops. Like I was saying, tell me all of *your* sorrows."

"Hey, how did you do that?" I asked, pulling at the edge of my bottle's blue Orangina label. "How'd you get a grip on yourself like that? I've never seen you so self-possessed. I'm impressed."

"It's part of what I'm going through with my new guru. Breathing exercises, positive mantras, a series of small adjustments to help me manage life's little obstacles. Being in the happy place really helps. I'm so glad you noticed, Flan."

"It was kind of hard not to notice."

"Right, well, I guess I'll be able to facilitate the exercise more smoothly with practice. The goal is to make seamless transitions from mood to mood and maintain a constant equilibrium."

"You might have a way to go before that," I joked. "But seriously, that's great. I could use some equilibrium myself."

"Right! Okay, therapy first. You play the crazy person for a change, and I'll listen and provide coun - sel."

"Ugh, okay," I said. "But it's probably going to sound totally stupid and unimportant."

"Nonsense, Flan. Now, hit me."

As I started to recount the many disasters of the trip for SBB, I did feel a little bit petty. I mean, here she was, having flown away from her movie—where she deals with struggles everyday that I can hardly begin to imagine—and I'm complaining about my lame high school social life?

But the more I talked, the more compassionate SBB became. I don't know if it was the happy place, or the proximity of a real friend, or the release of just saying all these words out loud, but pretty soon, I had unleashed the whole ugly story. From seventh grade and spin-the-bottle all the way up to Meredith and Judith totally bailing out on me—and my fears that all of it was my fault.

SBB didn't make me feel stupid, or petty, or any of the things that I was worried I was being. She just listened to my entire exhausting story, and at the end of it all, she sighed.

"Girls are tough, aren't they?"

"Yeah." I nodded.

"You know, I never had to deal with all of this high school drama. You see it on the movies, and it all looks so romantic, but—"

"Romantic? It's not romantic at all."

"Of course it is. You can't see it now, but this is enriching your character, Flan. It's almost like dealing with a broken heart. It's painful and traumatic in all sorts of ways, but figuring out who your true friends are is also an important part of growing up. I envy you, Flan. I'm sorry that this is happening on your vacation, but there will be plenty of vacations. You may only get this valuable life lesson once."

"But what does that *mean*? That I should just sit back and let Kennedy steal all of my friends?"

"People like Kennedy can only rule the roost for so long." She closed her eyes. "I predict her reign of terror cannot last." She opened one eye and winked at me.

"Now you're a fortune-teller?" I asked.

"I've been told I have clairvoyant eyes."

"Thanks for coming," I said. "I really needed to see a friend today."

"I know you did," she said. She retied the scarf around her neck and put her aviator glasses back on. "I hate to say it, but I think my work here is done. What I wouldn't give to linger in Nevis! Damn that workaholic Roderickson!" Then her Zen composure came back, and she smiled at me politely. "Take care, my love, and think about how strong you'll be after this trip."

And with that, she dashed back to her plane, where Luke patiently helped her get onboard. We blew each other kisses until she took off. And there I was, left standing on the beach by myself.

After a minute, I headed back toward the happy place, which was wonderful, but no substitute for the real SBB.

Whoa!" Meredith said when she came back, all wind-blown, from her yacht cruise that Tuesday afternoon. She stared up at the steamer trunk in the living room and said, "Who moved in?"

"Oh, Sara-Beth stopped by," I said, trying to sound nonchalant.

"Oh *man*! I can't believe I missed her." When Meredith and Judith first met SBB, they were so starstruck that they could barely talk to her. By now, Meredith was pretty comfortable around her, but she was always overly eager to hear about our hangouts. I knew that if there was one person Meredith was more stuck on than Kennedy, it was SBB. "Did you guys have so much fun?" she asked.

"So much fun," I said. "You should have seen it— her plane landed right on the beach outside our bungalow."

"Ohhh," she whined. "I wished I'd been around."

Hmph!

"Yeah, she was telling me all about what it's like to work with Jake Riverdale on the new movie. Apparently, he's a total disaster." I felt a little guilty rubbing it in, but I couldn't really help myself.

"So jealous of you right now, Flan." She stepped around the steamer trunk. "Is she still here? Do you guys have something awesome planned for tonight? 'Cause I was thinking—"

"Actually, she had to jet. They're trying to wrap up the last few scenes. She just left the trunk as a little souvenir." It felt strangely good to tell Meredith something that impressed her. The past couple of days, when we actually *had* been hanging out, she'd been so dismissive that I'd almost forgotten that she used to consider me someone who was worth talking to.

"Kennedy said I should invite you to the beachside dinner party tonight," she said.

"Um . . ." I stalled. The way she said it bugged me. *Kennedy said.* . . . How nice that Kennedy gave Mere - dith her permission to include me.

"We both figured you'd have plans already, but she said to do my best to bribe you to come." Meredith sat down next to me. "I think she's trying to reach out to you but doesn't know how, so she's using me to sort of . . . mediate?"

"Did she say that?"

"Not exactly, but . . ."

I sighed. Maybe SBB was right. There was no use starting World War III. I should focus on the things I could control—like my own experiences on this trip, not anyone else's. I definitely wasn't going to blow off the only offer I had. If Kennedy wanted to be bitchy, I could just ignore her, right? And consider it part of the growing experience?

"Sure," I said. "I'd love to come."

"Yay!" Meredith said, and she sounded genuinely happy. "I need some Flan time. Especially since Judith pooped out, us Stuy girls have to stick together, right?"

I nodded and smiled and offered her the first shower—again—but what I was thinking was, *am I really cut out to be a Stuy girl? Am I really cut out to "stick together" with Meredith?*

I caught a glimpse of myself in the steamer trunk mirror: sitting on the couch, slumped over with a scowl on my face. Gosh, if I had been looking like this all trip, I wouldn't want to hang out with me, either!

I sat up straight, put on a smile, and took a few deep breaths. It was amazing what it did for my appearance in the mirror, and it made me feel a lot better inside, too. Maybe this was what SBB was talking about when she referred to "minor adjustments." I felt a major attitude adjustment coming on. So what if the first twenty-four hours of the vacation had sucked? Maybe we were just getting started.

After Meredith finished in the bathroom, I took a shower and let my hair air-dry in the warm sea breeze. I put on my favorite Hollywould sequined flip-flops, a black Michael Stars tank top, and black hot shorts to show off my tan. I rooted through the steamer trunk to see what spoils SBB had left in there and found a bottle of this really pretty pink Benefit highlighter that, when dotted on the bridge of my nose and my cheekbones, made me look super sun-kissed and refreshed.

I even shared some of it with Meredith, who came out wearing a crazy kimono with her curly hair in a high bun.

"Whoa, Flan!" she said. "You look like a sun goddess. Don't stand next to me tonight, or I'll look way too pasty!"

"There," I said, dotting some highlighter on her cheekbones. "Your inner sun goddess has been released. *Now* will you stand next to me tonight?" I joked.

"Flan, you're the best. I'm so glad you brought me on this trip with you. There's nowhere I'd rather be."

For a second, I fought the urge to say *speak for yourself*. But then I just smiled and said, "I'm starving. Let's hit the beach."

We found the long white banquet table set up on the beach outside the bungalow where TZ was staying with his cousin, Rob. Rob had floppy brown hair and a great tan and, in the looks department alone, he kind of reminded me of Bennett.

The table was set for twelve, and I recognized a lot of the same kids from last night. I waved to Rena, and the real Paul came over and gave me a high five.

"Glad you came to the party," he said. "Where's your friend Judith?"

"Oh," I said, trying to figure out how to spin this one. "She had to go back to New York. Family issues."

"Bummer," Paul said, his blond locks falling over his eyes.

It *was* a bummer. It seemed like Paul had a little thing for Judith. I really wished she'd stuck around—especially because, from the looks of it, this party would have been a good chance for her to kick back and have a blast.

"I love how everything is so chic here," Meredith whispered at my side.

There were two men in black Speedo bathing suits,

tuxedo shirts, and bow ties who came by to take our drink orders.

I actually thought it was pretty campy, but I just nodded and smiled at Mer.

TZ appeared out of nowhere and put one arm around us both. I almost jumped back, I was so surprised to find an arm around me that wasn't Adam's.

"Please ignore the scantily clad men who are bringing you your Pellegrinos, ladies. My mother thinks they're *chic*."

I narrowly avoided snorting out my Pellegrino, and I heard Meredith change her tune and mutter something derogatory about their uniforms. I guess TZ seemed to find whatever she said hilarious and endearing, though, because he laughed and kissed her on the cheek.

"Love this girl," he said.

"Where's everyone sitting?" I said, breaking away from the smooch fest.

I noticed the table was arranged with large sand dollars at each place setting that had our names printed on them to indicate the seating arrangement.

When we sat down, I was sandwiched between Meredith and Rob. Rob ended up being super shy, and I made it my pet project to get him to talk and even laugh a little bit at dinner.

"So, what's your favorite part of Nevis so far?" I asked him.

He leaned in to me. "This is sort of embarrassing, but I took the best nap ever today on a hammock. I never get to take naps anymore. I felt like I was in preschool."

"Oh my God, I know," I said, trying to dismiss the nightmare I'd had yesterday about Kennedy. "Naps are a vacation necessity. Tomorrow we should schedule a group nap time and just line up the hammocks."

This seemed to embarrass Rob, because he just blushed and said, "Cool."

But we laughed and dug into our mahimahi seviche. Maybe it was because Kennedy was sitting at the other end of the table, but I was finally able to get over my Nevis issues and just enjoy myself.

Around the time they were serving us the crème brulée, I was realizing how quickly the night was flying by, and I knew that I didn't want it to end. The whole table laughed when TZ asked a waiter if he could try on his uniform and again when Kennedy did an impression of Mrs. Zumberg falling over herself drunkenly to flirt with "the help."

Sure, it was kind of mean, but that was Kennedy's sense of humor. When you were on the inside, it was hilarious. It was just when you were on the outside of her jokes, or worse, the brunt of them that—wait, I wasn't thinking about that tonight. Tonight was about crème brulée and starlight and the perfect sound the water made when it crashed up against the shore. I laughed to myself when I realized that I'd just unintentionally SBBed myself out of a funk.

After dinner, we sat in a cluster on the beach, and Rob brought out his guitar. He didn't talk much, but he sure could sing.

"Free Bird!" a guy with dreadlocks named Josh jokingly called out. "You never sing 'Free Bird' anymore."

"Yeah," TZ said, "and what about your excellent rendition of the 'Thong Song'?"

Rob made a gagging motion and started to play some old Neil Young stuff that I'd heard my dad play at home. It was totally mellow and a perfect choice for the mood.

The moon was so bright that we didn't need a fire, and I noticed that Kennedy and TZ were each wearing one of Meredith's necklaces. I guess she felt the *need* to make two more this afternoon. But actually, it was kind of cool to feel linked to the group because we were all wearing the necklaces together.

Finally, we were all on the inside.

When the singing was done, the boys insisted on

giving all the girls piggyback rides home to their respective bungalows. Actually, it was entirely TZ's idea, but I think Rob kind of got into it when he hoisted me up on his back.

The whole clan of us laughed all the way home.

When we got to our front door, TZ whispered something in Meredith's ear, and she nodded. Rob shuffled awkwardly next to me.

"Did you have fun tonight?" he asked.

"So much fun," I said.

"Good," he said. "I was hoping you were having fun."

I hadn't told Rob that I had a boyfriend—not that I thought he'd ever try anything with me. He was way too shy and a little too young for my taste (read: my age). Still, he'd been fun to hang out with for a night.

"Well," TZ said, "I guess this is goodnight. You girls want to kick it on the beach behind our place tomorrow? Say around noon?"

"Perfect," I said, and Meredith nodded enthusiastically.

A few minutes later, the two of us were standing in the bathroom washing our faces before we parted ways at our bedroom doors.

"So," I said. "You and TZ?"

"*Shhh,*" she said. "I don't want to jinx it. Nothing's happened yet. But omigod, how hot is he?"

"He's hot," I agreed. But it wasn't like Meredith to hold out on me. Usually she'd be spilling any details about even the most minuscule encounter with a guy. *Omigod, he asked to borrow a pencil. What do you think it means?*

Now she yawned dramatically. "Sooo tired. If I don't pass out in ten seconds, I think I'll fall asleep standing up."

"Sure," I said. "Well, good night."

I got in bed and lay there for a minute with the light on. I wasn't actually that tired. I thought about how much fun I'd had that night, how easy it was just to sit back and not get stressed about the little things that could have annoyed me. Kennedy was going to be the way she was going to be, and there was nothing I could do about it. I was glad that at least Mer and I were on better terms. It was going to make the rest of the week a whole lot easier.

I turned off the light and settled in to finally get some peaceful sleep.

But about three minutes later, I heard the very slow creaking of a footstep on a floorboard. Then another, and then another. It was Meredith heading down the hall.

Where was she going?

Before I could get up and out of bed, I heard the back door click behind her. By the time I got to the window to look out, I could only see her curly hair flying everywhere as she ran down the moonlit beach.

Chapter 13

The next morning, I made myself sit in the happy place. I tried to smile, even though I didn't feel like smiling. I tried to make minor adjustments in my attitude and physique. I even tried calling my parents, but they must have unplugged their bungalow's phone.

Still, even after all those efforts, I felt totally betrayed by Meredith. Worst of all, I felt ashamed of myself. It was embarrassing to remember how I had thought everything was going so well last night just because I had the approval of a few high-and-mighty private school kids.

And the thing with Meredith was really wigging me out the most. What had happened to her? In two days, she'd turned into a completely different person.

I waited for her to get home from her wild night out. I sat at the kitchen table, twiddling my thumbs.

After a while, I got up and looked in the fridge, but my stomach churned at the thought of food. I twiddled my thumbs some more. I texted SBB.

SABOTAGED. REIGN OF TERROR CONTINUES. GETS WORSE.

But as soon as I sent it, a wave of guilt rushed over me, and I sent her a follow-up text.

NO NEED TO FLY OUT. JUST WANTED TO VENT.

She was such a good friend, and I didn't want to start taking her gracious overtures for granted. Still, I *did* want her to write back with some sage advice. And I knew when I was thinking of her advice as sage, I was really in trouble.

Ten minutes later, I gave up waiting for her response, because I realized I'd been staring at my phone, whose wallpaper was a picture I'd taken of Judith, Meredith, and me standing in front of Out of the Kitchen!, our favorite dessert spot. *Ugh!* I deleted the picture and switched to a display of a particularly cute picture of Noodles wearing black Marc Jacobs sunglasses.

Much better. Back to thumb twiddling.

It was only eight in the morning, but I'd already been waiting for an hour. I slumped over the kitchen table and moped. I couldn't help but imagine what TZ must have whispered in Meredith's ear last night, right before we all said goodnight. I'd been on such a high at the time that I didn't even think too much about it. But now, my mind was swimming with unpleasant possibilities.

Just wait till she's asleep, and then the rest of us can start having fun.

Just like Kennedy always says, she's so unchill.

Lose the charity case and meet me on the beach.

"Please shut up!" I shouted out loud to myself.

"Uh, Flan, are you okay?"

Slowly, I lifted my head off the table. It was Meredith. She was standing in the kitchen doorway, looking a little bit afraid of me. She kind of had good reason to be. I was definitely acting a bit crazy.

"Where were you last night?" I asked, feeling both embarrassed for having to call her out and indignant that she was pretending nothing was wrong.

"What do you mean?" she said. Her voice sounded an octave higher than normal. "I was with you. Dinner on the beach? Remember?" She giggled. It was a pretty fake and unbecoming sound.

"You know what I mean," I said. I couldn't believe she was lying to me. "I heard you leave in the middle of the night. Where'd you go?"

"Nowhere. I just stepped outside for a minute. Fresh air, you know. I couldn't sleep." She shrugged and started pouring herself a bowl of Kashi.

"You stayed out all night."

"No, no, I didn't." She was stuttering—a terrible liar. She fumbled while closing the box of cereal, and I watched the color rise in her cheeks. "I probably just got up earlier than you did this morning," she said. "I went for a walk."

"Meredith, what are you doing?" I asked, pulling myself up to sit on the counter next to her. "Since when do you have to lie to me?"

"Since when do you interrogate me and make me feel like I'm a jailbird under your watch?"

I sucked in my breath. *What?*

"I didn't mean it like that," she said quickly. "I just . . . crap . . . Flan, the truth is, Kennedy wanted to go—"

I threw up my arms in the air. "Of course, *Kennedy wanted to go . . .*"

"She made me promise to keep the group super small. The kayak only held five people, and I didn't want to hurt your feelings. I just thought it'd be easier if I didn't tell you. I didn't mean for this to happen."

I watched Meredith grasp for words and could see how miserable this was making her feel. Suddenly, it was easy for me to see that the problem wasn't that Meredith was actively trying to exclude me. The problem was just that she could be a little spineless and would probably have a really hard time standing up to Kennedy. My anger subsided, just a tiny bit, and I started to feel more sorry for Meredith than anything else.

"You're going to get hurt," I said to her. As I said the words, I felt like Meredith's older sister, and I wanted to save her before she made the same mistake I'd made with Kennedy.

"What are you talking about?" she said. She was looking at herself in the mirror, repositioning her curls on her head.

"Kennedy is going to hurt you, Meredith. That's just what she does. You don't know who you're dealing with. Maybe it's all glamorous and exciting today, but I'm telling you, you're in way over your head."

Meredith's eyes got all squinty, and she took a step in my direction, pointing her finger at me.

"I get it. You're jealous."

"Meredith," I said, shaking my head.

"Admit it. You can't stand that I'm having fun here, and you're not. That I'm popular here, and you're not."

We stared each other down. This was a little intense for an early morning confrontation. Finally, I was the one who looked away.

"Sure, okay, yes," I said. "I wish I were having as much fun on this trip as you are. I don't think there's anything wrong with that. But what I'm saying to you doesn't have anything to do with being jealous. I know from experience that Kennedy is not a good friend. I just don't want to see you make the same mistake I made."

Meredith rapped her nails on the table. I could see goose bumps rising on her arms.

"Did you ever think that your mistakes and your experiences turned out the way they did for a reason? That maybe I don't need advice from someone who had to switch schools because she lost all of her friends?"

Ouch. I took a step back, reeling from her words. I didn't even know what to say back. Since when did Meredith have a biting mean streak in her? I was just trying to help.

Maybe it was time for me to face the facts. If Meredith had crossed over to the other side—as witnessed by her newfound major bitchiness—then there was nothing else I could do.

I stood up from the table, went into my room, and closed the door behind me. Meredith slammed her own door, followed by all of the drawers in her dresser. Her cell phone rang, and I tried to block out the conversation, but she seemed to be shouting just for my benefit.

"Oh *heyyy*, Kennedy. Long time no talk, right? Ha! I know . . . I'm getting ready right now. We're going to look *so* hot with braids."

She paused, and I shook my head at the image of Meredith with cornrows in her hair. Her bone structure was all wrong. A friend would warn a friend against such a possible style misstep. But were we friends anymore?

Her phone conversation with Kennedy continued.

"Who, Flan? No, of course she doesn't have plans . . . don't worry, I'll go out the window if I have to."

I made a face at Meredith through the wall and at Kennedy through the phone. How could someone be so evil that her evilness could rub off on someone as innocent as Meredith?

A few minutes later, she jetted off to have her hair braided, and I was still lying on my bed staring at the ceiling. My phone buzzed. SBB.

Hallelujah.

A real friend had come to my rescue. I opened my in-box and read her text message.

THEN IT COMES TO THIS. YOU MUST FIGHT THE GOOD FIGHT. STEAL THE QUEEN BEE'S HONEY—HER MAN.

I stared at the screen for a while and just took it in. Hmm. Not entirely logical, and not entirely written in the modern English vernacular (was SBB suddenly filming a gladiator movie?), but at least her text was something.

Sure, going after anyone's love interest, especially when I had a love interest of my own (hmm, I should really call—or maybe text—Adam, shouldn't I?) wasn't really my style. But then again, being treated this way wasn't really my style, either.

Maybe it was time to stop playing nice and rational, Flan Flood–style.

Maybe it was time to get even.

Chapter 14

*H*ere's the thing about TZ.

As confident and aesthetically perfect and seemingly intimidating as he was, I'd practically been raised on boys like him. It was one of the many advantages of having the type of older siblings that I had.

For as long as I could remember, Patch and Feb had been bringing their friends over to hang out at our place. At first, I hardly noticed them. I was too busy building pillow castle forts in our living room to take note of the future models, DJs, and socialites playing poker with Patch in my kitchen.

But I do remember the first time I did see one of the guys as something more than just an obstacle on my way to the refrigerator. It was my first day of sixth grade, and when I came home, a whole crew was hanging out in our breakfast nook, tearing through a pepperoni pie from John's Pizza.

144

Patch's friend Arno tugged on my ponytail and showed me his cards.

"What do you think, kid?" he asked. He nodded in Patch's direction. "Think he's got me?"

Most girls might have faltered, stuttered, or blushed. Arno was one of the best-looking freshman guys at Gissing, and his father owned the most prestigious gallery in Chelsea. But I wasn't most girls. I just grabbed the last slice of the pie and said, "Patch is bluffing. Hold 'em."

A slew of low whistles went around the table. Patch told me to get a life and leave his friends alone, but Arno just nodded at me, kind of in awe, and said, "Wow, where did *you* come from?"

Playing it cool with these guys was never something I had to think too hard about. Okay, I admit I wasn't completely consistent—sometimes I acted pretty goofy—but the point is that most of the time I didn't. And these guys really were older, cooler, and better-looking than most of the guys in the Abercrombie catalogs that most girls—Meredith included—probably grew up drooling over.

If Meredith ducked into the janitor's closet over a guy like Jules, would she even know what to do with a guy like TZ?

I, on the other hand, had been groomed for this.

As soon as I heard Meredith leave the bungalow, I knew what I had to do. I pulled my hair up into a high ponytail (my ex-boyfriend Jonathan used to say that the height of a girl's ponytail was directly proportional to how fun she was—the higher the ponytail, the more she could party). I raided SBB's steamer trunk again for makeup options, and actually found a Stila cosmetic case called Beach Chic Chic. It was full of shimmery gold stuff that looked super feminine and natural. I also grabbed a hot pink string bikini from SBB's trunk and pulled a short, white bubble skirt over it. I slid on my white flip-flops and looked in the mirror.

It was so not my normal, casual, New York–sleek style. I looked like I was going out on the prowl . . . and in a way, I was. Of course, I wasn't going to actually *do* anything—I'd never betray Adam. Catching TZ's attention—scratch that, *monopolizing* his attention—had nothing to do with wanting him for myself. It had everything to do with reminding Kennedy and Meredith that they weren't the only girls on this island.

I trooped down to the beach. I wasn't totally sure what I was going to do when I found TZ, but I was confident that my improvisation skills and flirtation prowess would come through for me in the clutch.

Soon, I found just the bronzed, shirtless guys I was

looking for. TZ, Rob, Paul, and a really built red-headed guy named Danny were playing beach volley-ball on the court outside of TZ's bungalow. I recognized a few of the poncho girls, who had spread out their towels along the sidelines. They were spraying tanning oil on each other, reading magazines, and trying to look like they weren't totally staring down the boys.

For a second, I thought about joining them. I was sure we'd discover we had mutual friends, and it wouldn't be such a bad idea to make a few more allies on this trip, now that my original crew had virtually dissolved. But making girlfriends wasn't part of today's mission, and I figured there'd still be plenty of time to make friends throughout the week.

"Operation Steal the Honey" had only one conquest, and his name was Terrick Zumberg.

I noticed a conveniently placed lifeguard stand close to where the boys where playing, and I positioned myself there until I could figure out an approach tactic. I pretended to unpack my beach bag while I caught the last few minutes of their game. After TZ spiked the ball over the net for the winning point, the boys took a water break.

"So, what's up with you and Kennedy?" Danny asked him. Danny was doing the move that really muscular guys do when they're trying to look down at their muscles all the time without looking like they're actually checking themselves out.

I froze. I was just within earshot, but from my spot behind the lifeguard stand, none of the guys had spotted me yet.

TZ shrugged his shoulders and grinned. His dark hair hung over his face, and he flung his head back to get it out of his eyes. I felt the tiniest flutter of butterflies in my stomach. Whoa. That wasn't supposed to happen. I shook it off. I needed my wits about me. I couldn't fall for his charm.

"Wait, is it Kennedy you're into?" Rob asked, putting some sunscreen on his neck. "Or is it Meredith?"

Exactly what I'd been wondering myself. *Which one is it, TZ?*

He laughed and said, "I'm weighing my options. You know, I don't want to jump into anything too quickly. Kennedy's cool, but she's the known quantity. Meredith's more of a wild card."

"Is that a good thing or a bad thing?" Paul drawled, surfer slow. "I can never tell with this dude."

TZ shook his head. "We'll see," he said. "We'll just have to see."

Hmm. So it didn't seem like he'd committed to either one of the girls yet—even though I wouldn't be surprised if both Meredith and Kennedy thought they already had TZ in their respective bags.

It looked like the boys were getting ready to play another game, so I figured it was now or never. I walked right up to them and flashed my biggest smile.

"Hey, guys," I said. "Can I play?"

"Hey, Flan!" Rob called.

TZ looked me up and down and gave me a sideways grin. "You sure you can play in that outfit?"

Whoops. I'd forgotten about that. Maybe this wasn't the best day to debut the string bikini. But letting on that I wasn't properly attired wasn't part of the plan. I just shrugged and said, "Sure, why not?"

Danny put his hand on my shoulder. "Perfect timing. I was gonna take a breather for this game anyway and chat up the hot girls on the beach towels over there."

"Dude, good luck with that one," Paul joked.

TZ turned to me. "Cool, you can be on my team."

"Cool," I said, feeling anything but. *Get a grip, Flan, get a grip.*

"Game on," TZ called.

Rob was on the other team, serving first. The ball came right to me, and I spiked it easily over to the other side.

"Nice," TZ called to me.

It was an intense game. There were more than a couple of times that TZ and I ended up diving for the same ball and getting just tangled enough for both of us to blush and apologize. In the end, we won by a point. Afterward, when we broke, he tossed me a bottle of water from the cooler.

"You looked good out there," he said.

"Thanks," I said, taking a long swig. "It felt good to play. A nice change from the estrogen overload alternative."

"Oh yeah," he said. "What's your crew up to today?"

"Nothing too exciting. I just wasn't up for getting my hair braided. I'd much rather hang out here and do something active."

"Yeah, you don't strike me as a total girly girl," he said. And for a second, I felt paranoid that what he meant was, *I can tell you have no friends*. But then he said, "I like that. So, what are you up to tonight?"

Crap. I needed cool plans, and fast. The only thing running through my head was the Zumbergs' itinerary tonight, which included watching the latest *Harry Potter* movie on a blown-up screen on the beach—and you didn't have to be a rocket scientist to know that TZ wouldn't want anything to do with that.

I bit my lip and racked my brain. And then, it hit

me—a stroke of brilliance. I looked just past TZ, along the beach horizon, and noticed a spectacular cliff overlooking the ocean. It was the prime spot for a really killer party, and it couldn't be more than half a mile down the beach.

Improvisational skills—check.

"Actually, I'm throwing a Hump Day party on that cliff," I said, gesturing behind him. "Right over there." Then I touched his chest with my pointer finger. "You'd better be there."

Flirtation prowess—check!

"Excuse me?" TZ laughed. "Hump Day?"

"You know," I said. "Wednesday—it's the hump of the week. A Hump Day party. My friends and I do it all the time at home." This was true—or at least, it used to be. Camille and I used to have Hump Day parties every Wednesday afternoon, complete with manicures, movies, and Moroccan food. But it'd been two years since our last one . . . ever since Kennedy moved to town. My venom for her surged again, and it got me through the rest of my made-up party story to TZ.

"Usually," I continued, "you're celebrating getting through the longest part of the week and looking forward to the weekend. But since it's not *too* much of a struggle getting through the days here in

Nevis"—okay, white lie—"we'll just celebrate the fact that we still have half the vacation left to party."

"Like a glass-is-half-full kind of Hump Day," TZ said, grabbing a towel and wiping his sweaty brow.

"Yeah," I said. "You got it."

"I like that," he said. "I'll be there. Who else are you inviting?"

"It'll probably be sort of small," I said. "But don't worry; it'll be exactly the group of people you'd want at a party like that."

"Sounds great," he said. "Because the alternative—getting stuck watching Harry Potter prance around with his wand—was looking grim." He gave me a high five.

I smiled at him. "I'll see you tonight."

"Hey, you don't want to hang out some more? Take a swim in the ocean or something?"

"I'd love to," I said. "But maybe another time? I have some last-minute things to take care of for to-night."

That was the understatement of the century. It was almost noon, and I had an entire event to plan from scratch in less than eight hours.

What had I gotten myself into?

*I*f I had a dollar for every time my sister said the words. "I once had a career as a . . ." I could probably buy the whole island of Nevis. In her twenty-two years, Feb's had stints as a personal shopper, a restaurateur, an MTV VJ, an investigative journalist (Page Six used to pay her to get them the dirt on where to find her celeb friends), a paralegal, and most recently, a party planner for the hip PR firm Harrison & Shriftman. She may have lasted only three days—she quit after a little spat with the boss over who was supposed to toast whose English muffin—but she did walk away with some very handy tips for how to plan an insta-party.

This week, Feb was staying on a different stretch of the beach a few miles away with a crew of the twentysomething kids. It was a long shot to think she'd be available this afternoon to help me navigate the planning of my own party, but I decided to give her a call. I flopped down on the living room couch in my bungalow and dialed her.

"You're blocking my sun," she said when she answered the phone.

"Hello?" I said, "Feb?"

"Oh, is that you, Flan? Sorry, I was talking to Davide. Honey, *move*. What can I do for you, Flan?"

"Who's Davide?" I asked. She pronounced the name *Dah*-vi-day.

"My boy du jour. He speaks no English. We met last night at Kirk's barbecue. You have to see the Roderickson place, Flan—it's fantastic. How are things at the kiddie camp?"

"Oh, you know," I said, looking around my lonely bungalow and taking a seat in the happy place. "Pretty good."

"Just pretty good?"

"I want to ask you a favor," I said, flipping on the small disco ball in the steamer trunk.

"You want to borrow my camel Manolo peep toe flats?" Feb asked.

"Actually, that too. But also, I'm trying to plan a really awesome party . . . in a really short amount of time. As in . . . tonight."

Feb sighed. "I swear, if you weren't my little sister . . . Okay." I could hear her sit up and start rummaging through her beach bag. I pictured her under a giant straw hat, behind huge sunglasses. She had the fairest skin in our fair-skinned family.

"Good thing I work best under pressure," she said. "Now what type of party are you thinking? I did a really great masquerade a few weeks ago, but I don't know if we could import the masks on such short notice. And everyone's pretty much over toga. Did you have a theme in mind?"

"Um," I said. This was not something I'd considered. And I had no idea that everyone was over toga. I didn't want to use the words Hump Day in this conversation for fear that Feb would misinterpret, and that'd only waste time. "I was just thinking . . . something fun? I don't know; what do you think?"

"Look, Davide's getting anxious to test out his new wet suit. I'm going to give you some phone numbers. You can get hors d'oeuvres and servers delivered in under three hours. The Zumbergs have their own DJ here this week, but you'll have to see if he's booked for one of their other parties tonight. And I know a man who does amazing things with lights on strings. What else? Let me think . . ."

"This is already really helpful, Feb. Thanks," I said.

I jotted down the numbers as she read them over the phone.

"Make some headway, and call me in a few hours." She paused. "I could be free tonight from midnight to one o'clock if you want me to make a cameo with friends and up your cool factor."

Feb was the only person I knew who could say that in all seriousness without sounding conceited. It was just, well, true. She practically oozed cool.

"Definitely," I said. "And bring Davide, so I can meet him."

"We'll see," she laughed. "You know how it is. Call me if you need any more help."

The afternoon flew by in a flurry of planning phone calls. I even arranged for a quick tasting to be delivered to the bungalow.

"Miss Flan?" a handsome, white-suited bungalow employee said when I opened the door.

"That's me," I said, eyeing the large white box he held.

"I hear you wanted to sample our selection of tropical tortes. I'm Guy, and I will be your guide." He pronounced his name *Ghee* and, when he took the lid off of the box, I gasped at all the brightly colored desserts inside.

"Begin with hibiscus," he said, pointing at the first in a line of desserts. They were so beautiful that they were (almost) too pretty to eat.

"Mmm," I said, swallowing my first bite. "*So* good."

The more desserts I tried, the more confused I got about which would go best with the jerk chicken kabobs we were having for dinner.

"You are having fun?" he asked me when my mouth was full of chocolate mousse.

"Oh yes," I said, swallowing. "This is great!"

"No, I mean, whole vacation? You are having fun?"

"Oh . . ." That took a little more thought to answer. "Yeah," I said finally, because, at the moment, things seemed to be looking up. "I'm having a really good time."

"Good," he said. "That's what I like to hear. Why don't I just tell the main kitchen to send all the desserts on a tray?"

I grinned and thanked him. "That's the best idea you could have had."

Next, I picked out a really cool lineup of music and dictated the wording for the invitations. I was having them sent out to the doorsteps of a select group of fifteen kids via a message in a bottle. Kennedy Pearson did *not* make the list.

Meredith came back to our place around five

o'clock, and when I heard her walking down our hallway, I found myself shutting the door to my bedroom. It was a motion that surprised me, because I was curious to see how her head o'braids had turned out.

But in that instant, I suddenly realized something important.

I knew I didn't want Kennedy at my party . . . but I kind of didn't want Meredith there either.

I couldn't believe I was making such a bold decision. I wasn't one to blatantly exclude my friends—even if I was pissed off at them. But this week had been such a nightmare, and I finally felt like I was gaining some control over my vacation destiny. I needed this party to go well. And I wasn't about to let either one of them ruin it.

I stayed in my room and lowered my voice as I made some last-minute phone calls. Meredith probably thought I was in there pouting, but really, I was trying on dress after dress (I sent a mental kiss to SBB for making me pack six dress options) to see which one matched the Manolo flats that Feb had sent over this afternoon. And at seven-thirty, *I* was the one sneaking out the window to avoid being seen by Meredith.

Half an hour later, the party was in full swing. Feb's connections totally delivered, and everyone was dancing to Jake Riverdale's new album under a colorful palm tree landscape strung with tiny shimmering white lights. Even though the music was awesome, I kept laughing when I remembered how annoyed SBB had been with JR when she'd visited. I could imagine her doing something crazy like throwing a coconut at my iPod to sabotage the music selection if she had been there right then.

But the music seemed to agree with everyone else, and within an hour, there was a huge pile of flip-flops in the corner. I took it as a good sign that everyone had to kick off their shoes so they could really get down on the sandy dance floor.

I stood back for a moment to survey the scene—and to nibble on some wasabi hummus–stuffed cucumbers and a lamb chop lollipop. I'd been right about the cliff—it was the perfect setting for a party.

"Oh my God, Flan, I love the star shaped fruit," Rena said, coming up and giving me a hug. She'd gotten a whole new slew of freckles since the first night I'd met her, and she looked really cute in her vintage Hawaiian print dress. "How did you cut them like this?"

"Babe, I really doubt Flan was spending all day with a paring knife and a pineapple." Paul laughed. He had his arm around Rena. Rumor had it that they'd hit it off late last night. For a second, I felt a little bummed about it—I guessed that Judith had missed her chance.

"Oh, right," Danny said, joining the convo. Of course, he was wearing another muscle shirt. "I'm sure Flan had a whole tribe of people working for her on this party."

I laughed when I thought of Guy's drive-by dessert delivery. "Just one very hard worker," I said. "Has anyone tried the smoothies?"

"Love the smoothies," I heard a voice behind me say. It was Mattie Hendricks, wearing jean shorts and a simple white T-shirt from the Gap. I was glad to see she'd made it out. "Thanks so much for inviting me, Flan. Your party is the best."

"Oh, I just threw it together," I said, feeling slightly guilty about how much I was enjoying being the center of attention.

One thing I wasn't feeling guilty about was Meredith. If it hadn't been for TZ, I might not have thought about her at all. It was the first time all week that I had felt worry free, and I was loving it.

"Where do you think they are?" TZ asked me after we had devoured some scallop seviche.

"Who?" I asked innocently, feeling the weight of their names in the pit of my stomach.

For a second, he looked at me like the answer was totally obvious. "Meredith," he said. "And Kennedy. Your friends? I thought you guys would have all come together."

"Yeah," Danny said. "Where are those two?"

I didn't know why I hadn't thought to prepare an answer to that question. Obviously everyone was going to want to know where they were. Kennedy had basically been the social director for the group since we arrived. No one would think the party was complete without them. Unless I could convince them to . . . .

"I don't know. I thought they'd be here, too," I found myself saying. "Maybe they're too cool to hang out with us. I'm not sure this party is exclusive enough for them."

I was waiting for someone to agree with me, for anyone to speak up and say that Kennedy was a tyrant and Meredith was a follower. But instead of jumping in and expressing how lame the two of them were for not showing up at this raging party, the crowd seemed to dissipate. I hadn't given them the answer they were looking for. And now everyone was looking toward the path that lead to the cliff.

Two figures were approaching the party. In the dusk, all I could make out were the silhouettes of two heads of braided hair.

I almost dropped my virgin daiquiri with its cute little pink umbrella.

Kennedy and Meredith were totally crashing my party.

TZ, Rob, and Danny all left my side and began jogging down the path toward the enemy.

"Meredith," TZ called out. "You made it."

It was pretty obvious at that point that she was the object of Terrick's affection. He was fingering her braids, and she was beaming up at him shyly. There was a time when I would have been ecstatic that Meredith was playing it cool with a really great guy, but now I just felt like crying.

"Hey, everybody," Kennedy called, confident as ever. "Guess what I scored for us?"

Suddenly the whole party was buzzing with the news that a forty-foot yacht with a sweet sound system was going to be picking us up in fifteen minutes for fireworks down by the cay.

The girls grabbed their bags and put their shoes back on. The guys polished off their drinks. I had never seen a party empty out so fast. Even the servers looked stunned. I didn't know what to do. I wasn't just going to stick around and let my party end with me standing alone in the middle of the dance floor.

So I followed them. Only minutes before, I'd been

calling Meredith a follower in my head, and now I was running after her, trying to keep up.

"Meredith," I called. "Wait up!" And then I felt so awful and awkward that I'd said that, and I knew for sure I was turning purple. But it didn't matter, because she didn't even turn around.

When we got to the water, Kennedy ushered everyone onboard. She stood at the entrance with Meredith, like a couple of bouncers, and I waited in the line, knowing exactly what was coming my way.

When I got to the front, Kennedy turned to me sweetly and said, "Hey, Flan, heard it was a *great* party. What are you up to now?"

I couldn't think of a single thing to say. I looked at Meredith, but she was looking down. Did they want me to ask permission to get on the yacht?

"I wish we could invite you to come with us now," Kennedy finally said with a smug grin. "But we're at capacity. Sorry!" She gave me a little shove, and I stumbled back onto the dock. With that parting signal, my party began to sail away.

My feet felt stuck to the dock. I stood there, feeling like a loser and a liar and a hypocrite, as I watched everyone else continue to have an awesome time on the boat.

And the worst part was, I knew I deserved it.

*T*welve hours later, I had dragged myself all the way up to the adult camp for the first time that week. It was a struggle to get out of bed—after last night, all I wanted to do was hide in the steamer trunk. But my whole family was supposed to meet for Thanksgiving brunch at one of the resort's restaurants. Before we all split up for our age groups' respective turkey dinners, I really needed some quality time with the people who had no choice but to love me unconditionally.

When I arrived at my parents' place, my mom greeted me at the door and flung her arms around me. "Perfect timing; I just finished watching the DVD of *Catch and Release*. Can *you* fit your whole fist in your mouth, Flan?"

"Huh?" I asked.

"Never mind. Of course my youngest, most responsible child is the first to arrive," she said. "Patch and

Feb swore they were on their way, but you know them. Anything could come up."

As my mother went on about her TV watching and tennis winnings and my father's crazy schedule that week, I stood still in her arms. It felt like it had been a long time since I'd been hugged.

"Flan? Are you okay?"

I gave her one last squeeze before I pulled away. "Uh-huh," I said. "I'm fine."

"Didn't your friends want to come to brunch, honey?" she asked me as she reapplied her Chanel lipstick.

I'd completely forgotten that it might look suspicious that Meredith and Judith weren't by my side.

"Oh," I stammered, "no. They wanted to sleep in a little bit."

I stepped inside and took a look around my parents' pad. If my bungalow was souped-up, theirs was mogul-worthy. They must have had ten thousand square feet of luxuriousness. There were personal side-by-side Jacuzzis on the deck and coconut trees lining the grounds.

When my dad got off his conference call, my parents and I walked to a pretty little restaurant in the town square called Café Anjou. We took our seats at a large table while we waited for Patch and Feb.

"Do these people even know how to run a business?" my dad shouted at no one. He kept putting down his Bloody Mary to manhandle his BlackBerry. Apparently, he was looking into the logistics of buying a place here on the beach.

"Rick, put down that monstrosity," my mother said. "It's a holiday."

"Mom, he's probably playing Tetris," Patch said, suddenly standing over us. He took a seat, and I couldn't believe how happy I was to see him. Even though he was technically staying at the kids' camp near me, I don't think he'd spent much time on the actual island this week. He and his friends were doing more island-hopping than itinerary-following.

"How's it going, kiddo?" he said to me. "You remember Emerald, right?" I scooted over my chair to make room at the table for Emerald Wilcox, who sometimes tagged along with Patch and Feb for low-key (relatively speaking) hangouts in between her recording sessions in L.A.

"Hey, Emerald," I said. "What's up?"

"Cool," she said. It was the only word I'd ever heard her say.

Just then, Feb came rushing into the restaurant on the arm of the tallest, darkest, and handsomest guy I'd ever seen. This had to be Davide.

"Hello, family," she said, swooping down to kiss us each on the top of the head like she was playing Duck, Duck, Goose. "Emerald, you made it! How was the fund-raising concert?"

"Cool," Emerald said, nodding.

I put out my hand to introduce myself to Feb's new man.

"You must be—"

"*Pierro,*" Feb said, cutting me off with a knowing look. "This is my little sister, Flan."

Pierro shook my hand. "Like you say," he said to Feb. "She is just as cute as button."

Feb laughed her fake boy-appeasing laugh and whispered to me, "At least this one speaks a *little* English. Cute, huh?"

"Very," I said.

"So last night was fun?" she asked, sitting down next to me. "I heard there were some kick-ass late-night fireworks off the cay. Your pre-party was probably the perfect way to start the night."

I opened my mouth to start to tell Feb . . . I didn't even know what. That I'd been ditched by the whole island? That my party was the laughingstock of Nevis? But luckily, I was saved by my mother's fork dinging against her mimosa flute.

"Hurry up and sit down, everyone. Pierro, there's

a spot right next to me." She gave him her hostess mom smile. "So. Now that everyone's together for at least five minutes, why don't we all go around the table and say what we are most thankful for?"

A chorus of groans from the rest of the family rang out around our table.

"I have a better idea," Feb said. "Let's talk about the sweet pad Dad's going to buy here. I'm totally going to have my wedding here someday."

"These a-hole brokers don't know crap," my dad muttered and slammed down his BlackBerry. This made everyone laugh, including my mom, who was probably still holding out for our roundtable Thanksgiving kumbaya.

It was such a relief to know that, no matter what crazy drama went down with my social life, I could always count on my family to be fabulous, if slightly insane. There'd been times this week when I felt as though I didn't have much to be thankful for, but now, surrounded by my family, I decided to clank my knife against my glass of sparkling OJ and say, "Well, I'm thankful for a lot of things."

My family turned to look at me. My mom's face lit up expectantly.

"Like a sister who can always come through with an amazing party plan."

Feb nodded at me and raised her glass. "Obvi," she said.

"And a brother who taught me how to hang with all different sorts of people—even if he won't let me in on his poker games."

Patch laughed and said, "I don't want to lose *all* my money."

Finally, I turned to my parents. "And I'm thankful for you guys, for giving me the chance to do my own thing this fall."

I could have gone on about how much it meant to me to know that they were there now, when I really needed some support, but I didn't want to get too sappy.

Still, it was just enough to make my mother burst into tears.

Feb turned to Pierro, who was looking a little started. "Don't worry," she said, refilling his mimosa with champagne. "She gets choked up at almost every family gathering. You get used to it."

After my mom blew her nose daintily into her napkin, she said, "Well, that was just about the best thing that I've ever heard. Now, who wants to share the Meyer lemon waffle with me?"

But Patch had a plane to catch, and Feb and Pierro had made an early reservation for a couples massage.

My dad was still doing the whole low-carb thing, so that left me at the table with my mom.

She eyed me as she cut into the waffle.

"You haven't gotten much color," she said.

I looked down at my arm, which seemed even paler than normal. "I guess I haven't been spending too much time outside."

She squinted at me. She could always see right through me.

"I don't know this Flan," my mother said, circling her fork in the direction of my face. "My Flan is a smiler; she's a sun goddess; she's the life of the party. Now, you know I appreciated your Thanksgiving message very much. But I didn't see *you* inside of it."

My mouth went dry. I opened it, but nothing came out.

My mom put her hand over mine. "Is it Kennedy? I saw her mother at the tennis courts the other day. If Kennedy's anything like I remember, she must be as nasty as ever."

I nodded miserably.

"Do you want to go home?" she asked me.

Until then, I hadn't really thought of that as an actual possibility. *Did* I want to leave? Wouldn't leaving the trip early be quitting?

"No," I said. "I don't want to leave. I just wish I didn't feel so out of place."

For a moment, we sat there chewing. I knew that my mom knew this was a bigger problem than just going home could solve. But neither one of us seemed to have a solution.

Just then, I felt two hands cover my eyes like a blindfold.

"Guess who?"

I knew the voice, but I couldn't . . . I just couldn't place it yet.

I tugged at the hands and turned around. Without thinking, my whole face lit up.

It was my old best friend, Camille.

Camille of the Kennedy friend theft, sure . . . but she was also Camille of the great bicycle race of fifth grade, of the annual Labor Day camping trip to Sag Harbor, and of the weekly Friday night sleepovers. She was Camille of the best-friends-forever necklace, which I still had in my jewelry box at home.

Her dirty blond hair had grown way past her shoulders. It was so thick and long and shiny that it seemed almost to take over her small frame. Her skin was still flawless, and her icy blue eyes were smiling at me as if we hadn't missed a beat in our friendship.

171

But it was crazy for me to feel that way—it'd been over a year since we'd really hung out.

"Hey, Flan," she said.

"Hey, Camille."

My mother gave me a nudging smile, and the two of us stepped out to the restaurant's courtyard to catch up.

"I didn't even know you were coming," I said.

"We weren't going to. My grandmother came to the city for the holiday, but when she found out we were skipping this trip for her, she insisted that we all fly down together." Camille pointed to an elderly lady through the window. She was sitting on a lounge chair surrounded by three old men. Each of them seemed to be vying for her attention.

"She's in heaven," Camille said, laughing.

"I'm *so* glad to see you," I found myself saying.

Camille nodded and looked down at her feet. "Me, too. It's been forever. I know things were weird last year, but I have to say they're definitely much weirder now that you're not around at all." She bit her lip. "So, how are you? I hear you're liking Stuyvesant a lot."

As I started to catch Camille up on my past few months at school, I couldn't help but feel like she laughed in all the right places, groaned in all the right places, and grabbed my hand impulsively in all the right places—usually when I was telling her about my boy escapades. I mean, I hadn't even remembered that there *were* right places until Camille and I started talking. She told me all the dirt on our old teachers and filled me in on whose party had been the most fun and the most lame so far this year.

And when she leaned in to whisper that she'd had her first real kiss the month before, I realized that she was the only girl I knew who didn't have to stand on her tiptoes to reach my ear. We were both an awkward five-foot ten!

"How come you make your growth spurt look so much less gawky than I do?" I asked her.

"Not even! You practically made the restaurant look like a runway when I followed you outside," Camille insisted.

And that was when I remembered: *this* was what it was like to have a best friend.

"Okay," she finally said when we'd gone through all the basic catch-up details. "Truth?"

"Truth," I said.

"I really miss you," she said. "I've thought about calling you a million times to make up, but seeing you now, I know that I should have done it so much sooner. Kennedy and I are barely even friends any-more. She thinks she rules the school. But everyone is totally fed up with her, and the problem is that none of us have figured out how to let her know."

I sighed. "*I'm* totally fed up with her," I said. "And I've only been around her for a few days. This vacation's been a disaster—well, until right about now."

Camille leaned in and gave me a giant hug. We stood there on the bustling patio, just laughing and hugging and laughing some more, not caring at all that we must have looked like professional dorks.

As we started strolling out of town to clock some beach sun time, Camille said, "So has it really been that bad this week? Don't tell me Kennedy's been trying to control this entire island."

"It's a reign of terror, island style."

"Well," she said, "what do you say we put a stop to that today?"

Camille gave me her megawatt wink, and I knew somehow that this week was about to get back on track.

Chapter 17

Camille and I decided that we would head down to the kids' Thanksgiving dinner together that night. The plan was to arrive at the restaurant overlooking the water at sunset. We'd heard that Bobby Flay's staff had flown down to cook deep-fried turkey and a huge buffet full of other Thanksgiving fare. The invitation said "dress to impress."

The two of us had spent the afternoon hanging out at my bungalow and picking out our outfits—both of us decided to wear complementary dresses from Diane von Furstenberg. We drank pomegranate spritzers, took a dip in the hot tub on the deck, and explored even more of the hidden compartments within SBB's steamer trunk.

"Oh my God," Camille said, keeling over with laughter when she opened a drawer to find it filled with three different-colored Magic 8 Balls, a Ouija board, and a fortune-telling book called *The Book of Answers*.

"What *is* all this stuff?" she asked.

"*This* is SBB," I laughed, peering over Camille's shoulder. "She's the only person on earth who trusts this kind of junk. She should totally buy stock in Ricky's NYC."

"I need to meet this girl," Camille said. "I think I'm going to love her."

Suddenly, I wished I could swap out Meredith for Camille as my roommate, but since Camille was only here for a few days, she had a smaller cabin attached to her parents' place up the hill.

"Where is Meredith anyway?" Camille asked when I showed her what could have been her room. "She didn't leave you a note? That's lame. What kind of a replacement best friend is she?"

I handed Camille a confirmation printout of a snorkeling trip I'd found. Meredith must have left it on the kitchen table.

"Do you think this is her way of letting me know that she wouldn't be around today, but that I didn't deserve a friendly note after the way I acted last night?"

"Oh, Flan," Camille said. "It couldn't have been that bad. It sounds like they got what they deserved.

Why should you have invited them if they were being so catty?"

"I know," I said. "I just wish it didn't have to be so juvenile—me pointing the finger and saying '*They started it.*' Regardless of who started it, I'm the one who came off looking like a total tool last night when everybody jumped on Kennedy's yacht."

Camille's eyes got wide. "I have an idea!"

I laughed. "You always have an idea. Remember the water balloon barrage in Mr. Topple's class?"

"Whatever! That was one of my best ideas in fourth grade! And this one's really good, too." She reached into her bag and pulled out two small silver objects shaped like turkeys.

"What are these," I asked, "earrings?"

"Oh my God, no! They're cookie cutters! But I'd love to see you try and wear them as earrings. My grandma gave them to me. You know how she lives for that stuff—anything shaped like a holiday, she buys it."

"You want to bake?" I said, still confused.

"*You* want to bake," she corrected. "We'll make turkey cookies for the whole crew tonight. Nothing makes amends like butter and sugar, right? We'll bring trays of them down to the restaurant. I have this recipe saved online for sugar cookies; they are sooo awesome when you dip them in cinnamon-chocolate fondue."

"Okay—but where are we supposed to get all the chocolate?"

"I think the pool boy at my parents' bungalow has a crush on me. I'll just give him a ring and see what he can do."

A few hours later, the two of us were seated next to each other at the long banquet table, watching the sunset. The cookies had come out super cute, and Camille was right—the one I sampled dipped in melted cinnamon-chocolate did have a certain *je ne sais quoi.*

We'd gotten a whole basketful of chocolate and a fondue pot from the pool boy, who turned out to be the same Guy who'd taken me on my whirlwind tour of desserts. Did that guy ever take a break?

"Be careful, girls," he said when he came by to deliver the chocolate bars. "Too much sugar can make a girl run wild." He winked, then disappeared.

Now we were safeguarding the chocolate in Camille's giant Whole Foods tote to unveil at the end of the meal.

It was just a fun dessert, but knowing that we had a big plate of cookies and yummy chocolate for everyone made me feel sort of on top of things, for a change.

I'd already prepped Camille on how to avoid Kennedy and Meredith when we got to the restaurant. I just wasn't ready to deal with them. But when we got there, the evil duo hadn't arrived yet. And without them, everybody just looked cool and laid-back.

Really, everyone was being incredibly nice—from one of the poncho girls who loved the Salt Works jeans I was wearing, to Rob, who didn't understand why I hadn't been at the fireworks last night.

For a second, I was stunned. Didn't they see how embarrassing last night had been for me? Was no one else aware of the drama that had gone down among Kennedy, Meredith, and me?

But no one even seemed to be fazed by it. As we hung out over appetizers of oyster stuffed bites and cranberry gorgonzola tarts, I came to a startling realization.

Everyone else was just as caught up in their own issues. No one even realized what a disaster of a trip this week had been for Flan Flood. Here I'd been, feeling so much in the spotlight, and suddenly, I discovered that the opposite was true. It was both a relief and a huge wake-up call.

But just before the sit-down dinner began, Meredith and Kennedy arrived—two people who definitely *did* know, and care, all about my drama. Kennedy blew past me, and Meredith gave me a sort of confused, guilty half-smile, but we stayed a comfortable distance away from each other.

The buzz was that TZ was hanging out with his family until dessert—which was just fine with me. I wasn't in any rush to face him after the way I'd acted last night.

When Meredith took her seat next to Kennedy at the other end of the table, Camille leaned in to me and said, "That's her, isn't it? I just don't know about her bone structure with those braids."

In that instant, I loved her even more completely. She wasn't saying it in an empty, bitchy way—she just shared my feelings about Meredith and wanted hair success stories for everyone she saw.

Dinner was delicious, and I only snagged Meredith's eye once. Both of us blushed and looked back down at our plates. Clearly, we had a conversation coming our way. But mostly, I tried not to think about it. Camille was making all of us laugh with her imitation of her grandmother flirting with all the old men at the pool.

On my right was Mattie Hendricks. She nudged

me at one point when we were all laughing at one of Camille's impressions and said, "Isn't this the most fun you've ever had?"

If I were to be honest with Mattie, I could give her a whole slew of reasons why this paled in comparison to the fun I had most of the time in the city. But she seemed so earnest and excited to be hanging out with us at this table that I just smiled at her and said, "Yeah, it's pretty awesome."

"Pretty awesome?" she said, adjusting her indigo headband. "It's *amazing*. You know how we were talking about TZ that first night at the bonfire?"

"Yeah," I said, wondering where this conversation was going. "I remember. Why do you ask?"

"I just about *died* when I realized he was going to be on this trip. My friends and I are all obsessed with him. When I texted them to say that he was staying two doors down from me this week, they all bet me that I couldn't get him to talk to me. I've been trying to get his attention all week."

I was about to open my mouth to tell Mattie that yeah, TZ was hot, but that I was sure she could find an equally awesome guy, and not to sweat it if things didn't pan out this week, when Kennedy came up behind us on her way back from a trip to the buffet.

"Did I hear that someone has a little crush on TZ?" she asked, her voice all high and saccharine.

Mattie blushed, but she couldn't contain herself. She grinned shyly at Kennedy. "No . . . I mean . . . I don't know."

"How much do you like him?" Kennedy asked. Her voice was louder than Mattie probably realized, and people at the table were looking at us. "Like, what would you do for the chance to go out with him?"

"I don't know," Mattie said again, squirming in her seat.

"Would you eat dog food if it meant you could kiss TZ?"

"Um," Mattie said. She was starting to look uncomfortable. Kennedy was getting really loud.

Now the whole table of twenty-five people was looking at us. Kennedy was being stupid and inappropriate, and I could tell Mattie had no idea what to do. I don't know why, but it was so much easier for me to stand up for her than it'd been for me to stand up for myself all week.

"Kennedy, why don't you leave her alone?" I said, twisting around to face her.

"She'd probably kiss Terrick's dog just to get close to him." Now Kennedy was practically shouting. "Wouldn't you, Mattie? Admit it."

"Kennedy," I said, matching her voice. "Shut up, okay? What are you trying to do?"

She turned to me, and I could see her eyes flashing. "What do you care, Flan? Now you're Mattie's baby-sitter?"

Before I realized it, I was standing up, facing the enemy, making a whole spectacle in front of the entire dinner party.

"You know what? You treat people like crap. I don't know why you do it, but I'm sick of just standing by and watching you. You can't act like this. It's not right."

Kennedy put her hands on her hips. "Oh yeah, well what's *right* by Flan Flood standards? If you're such an expert on friendship, then why don't you tell everyone here why one of your best friends jumped ship on day two of this vacation, and your other best friend can't even stand to be near you? She hasn't slept at your bungalow in days."

I sucked in my breath and found myself looking at Meredith across the table, but she wouldn't return my gaze. Then I realized that this wasn't about Meredith. This was only about Kennedy's struggle for power.

Just then, the door to the restaurant opened up and TZ sauntered in with an apple pie and a jug of sparkling cider. "Courtesy of Mom and Pop Zumberg," he said. "Who's ready to get this party started?"

Kennedy rushed to him and whispered something in his ear. "Let's get out of here," she said aloud. "This dinner blows. It's time for the non-losers to get out and have some fun."

I braced myself for the mass exodus à la last night to occur. But I'd forgotten how much it meant to have a real friend waiting in the wings. While I'd been duking it out with Kennedy, Camille had been knowingly distracting everyone with our secret weapon: the cookies and cinnamon-chocolate.

By the time I'd turned around, fully expecting the rest of the table to have thrown down their napkins to duck out with Kennedy, Camille had the whole room dipping cookies in chocolate and saying cheers to each other before they swallowed them down.

TZ walked right over and gave Camille a hug. As it turned out, they were old family friends and were totally psyched to see each other.

He picked up a cookie and dunked it in the chocolate. "Damn," he said after he had taken a bite. "You two made these? You should open a store in the city. These cookies are amazing!"

I was so stunned that TZ didn't hate me that I almost didn't notice Kennedy fuming.

"*Okaaay*, who wants to go down to the beach? I think I can get us the yacht again." But she sounded hesitant and nervous. I tried not to take too much satisfaction in the shakiness of her voice.

"Danny, Rob, come on. I know you guys are in," she said.

And at that moment, both Danny and Rob grabbed cookies from our pile and dipped them in our chocolate.

"Dude," Rob said, "I think we're cool to hang out here."

"Whatever," Kennedy said, clearly pissed. "Meredith, let's go."

Meredith stood up from her seat at the table. I watched her lay down her turkey cookie without taking a bite and follow Kennedy out of the room. The braids looked terrible on her. I should have been there to stop her from getting them in the first place.

Even though the turn of events tonight had been awesome, I couldn't help but feel a tinge of sadness as the clinking sound of Mer's beaded braids disappeared down to the beach.

Chapter 18

After midnight, a big group of us moved the party down to the beach. Rob was wearing a Rasta wig and playing the guitar again. A few people were racing each other down the sandbars. The bonfire was lit, and we were all passing around s'mores.

"We should do something to celebrate the fact that this party is drama-free," Camille said, grinning at me.

TZ laughed and speared another marshmallow. "Aren't we already?" he asked. "What's not celebratory about tonight?"

"I mean we should do something *crazy*," Camille said, waving her hands in the air.

"Just say the word," TZ said. "I'm all about the crazy celebrations."

It was obvious that everyone was having an awesome time—even Mattie had taken off her loafers and dipped her feet in the water for a few seconds—but I was still surprised that TZ didn't seem to mind that Kennedy and Meredith weren't hanging out with everyone else.

"TZ, do you know what Kennedy's up to tonight?" I asked him.

"Oh, you girls and your drama," he said, patting my knee.

"I didn't mean it like that. I just, I thought you guys were friends. I thought you and Meredith were . . . friends, too."

"Look, Kennedy's one story. Part of me loves her. I mean, we go back to when we were in diapers. So I know we'll always be cool. But sometimes she can just be too intense. I'm so not into all that exclusivity bullshit—especially not on vacation."

"Yeah," I said, "that makes sense." But I still had to know one more thing. "What about Meredith?"

"I like Meredith. I think she's really cute. Okay, not as cute as the present company." He nudged Camille's and my knees and gave us his trillion dollar smile. "And she seemed cool, you know, really mellow. Then, once I started talking to her . . . I don't know, sometimes it seemed like she didn't know who she was, like she was just agreeing with whoever was talking, regardless of how she really felt. I like a girl who knows what she wants, even if I totally disagree with her."

I nodded and withdrew my marshmallow from the fire. It was burned to a crisp, just the way I liked it.

TZ pointed at my flaming 'mallow. "Like that right there. I wholeheartedly disagree with the way you have destroyed your s'more."

"Destroyed!" I said, acting shocked. "You haven't lived until you've tasted my singed s'more specialty."

"Oh, really," he joked. "I assume you'll be serving those at your cookies-and-chocolate shop on West Fourth Street?"

"It'll be the daily special," I said.

We grinned at each other, and for a second neither one of us said anything. The heat of the fire on my face suddenly felt super intense.

"Okay, you two, I'll settle this," Camille said. "Give me both of your s'mores, and I'll be the judge of whose is more delicious."

"That's clearly just a ploy to get more s'mores without having to do any of the work," TZ said. But in the end, both of us handed them over.

Camille sampled the s'mores with the attention to detail of a judge on *Top Chef*. After a pensive moment, she deemed mine superior in chocolate meltiness and TZ's superior in marshmallow-to-graham cooperation.

"That's a cop-out," TZ said. "You're just afraid to pick your favorite."

"Not even," Camille said, feigning a diva and shaking her finger at us. "Unlike Meredith, I have never in my life been scared to have an opinion."

"Oh, Meredith." I sighed. I wondered what she was doing right now. "She was a good friend. I just think she has some growing up to do."

"Along with a little bit of jewelry-making training," TZ said, rubbing his neck. He was still wearing her necklace. I had stopped wearing mine days ago. But then he said, "What'd she weave this thing out of, poison ivy? My neck is on fire. I have to get rid of this."

At that moment, TZ's border collie trotted over to us and nuzzled up against Camille.

"Hey, Bruce," she said, giving him a scratch. "Bruce, do you need a new collar? TZ, give me that thing."

TZ tossed her the necklace, and she fastened it around the poor dog's neck. Bruce tried to get at his neck to give his new collar a sniff, but he couldn't reach it, so he just gave us a few angry barks and trotted off.

"I think it suits him," Camille said thoughtfully.

"Well, that's because he's got terrible taste," TZ said. "Yesterday, I took him for a walk up on the cliff over there, and he was getting all flirty with this poodle—"

"Um, I have a crazy beyond crazy idea," Camille suddenly butted in.

"Yay!" I said. There was something so genuine about Camille that it was hard not to get just as excited as she was, even before I had a clue what she was talking about.

"What is it this time?" TZ joked. He looked at me. "Are you familiar with her *ideas*?"

I laughed. "They're practically legendary around my house. My mother still can't get the garlic smell out of her Persian rug from one of Camille's ideas back in third grade."

"No, you guys'll like this one. TZ, which cliff did you take Bruce for a walk to yesterday?"

TZ pointed out in front of him. "That one right there. Star Cliff. The one where Flan . . ."

He trailed off, but I could have finished his sentence in a number of ways.

The cliff where Flan was mortally mortified.

The site of Flan's botched party.

The place no friend of Flan's would bring up if he wanted to avoid her extreme embarrassment.

Camille jumped in to my rescue. "You mean the one where Flan, and you, and me are going to go right now to go cliff-diving until sunrise?"

"Whoa," TZ said, "where did that come from?"

"Come on. Haven't you always wanted to do that?"

The truth was, I *had* always wanted to do that. Ever since I read an article in my dad's *Extreme Adventure* magazine four years ago. It was one of my major life-time fantasy goals, and the only person who knew that was . . . Camille!

I grinned at her. "Seriously," I said.

"Seriously."

TZ shrugged. "I guess we can sleep when we're dead."

Pretty soon after that, the party started to break up. Everyone's eyes were bloodshot from staring at the fire for so long, and people were yawning, clearly crashing from their sugar highs.

On the other side of the bonfire, Rena shouted, "Can we please stop listening to Amy Winehouse? I think I'm about to shoot myself."

"What are you talking about?" Paul called back. "It's been Rob playing guitar the whole time."

Camille and I giggled.

"Ouch," TZ whispered to me. "I know my cousin has kind of a high voice, but man. I hope he didn't hear that."

"Whatever, you guys," Rob said, slinging his guitar over his back. "I'm going to turn in. Don't be asking me for autographs when I have a platinum album."

Danny raised his voice an octave and squealed, "Can you make this one out to Danny, from Amy with love?"

Everyone was laughing and in good spirits as they packed up their stuff and got ready to head home. The boys snuffed out the bonfire using their very macho method of peeing on it and then dousing it with seawater when that didn't work.

Camille, TZ, and I hung back after we said good night to the rest of the crew.

"So, are we really going to do this?" TZ asked.

"Yeah," I said, taking control. "We are."

"Okay." He put his arm around me. "Whatever Flan says goes."

It was just about five in the morning when the three of us got to the summit of the cliff. We'd been having so much fun on the walk up that I forgot what kind of spectacular view was awaiting us at the top. When we'd started walking, there'd been the faintest tinge of yellow in the sky. The cliff faced east, and by now the eastern sky was streaked a brilliant orange-red. A few clouds gathered along the horizon and glowed hot pink in front of the sun.

"When was the last time you were up to see the sunrise?" TZ asked us.

"Fishing trip with the dads, sixth grade," Camille

and I both said at the exact same time. Then we burst out laughing.

"Jinx!" she shouted.

"That trip was amazing," I said to Camille.

"Remember when you caught that massive flounder, and your dad made us eat it for dinner?" Camille said.

"Gross!" I said, remembering.

"Flounder's awesome," TZ said. "The three of us should go fishing sometime. I could show you guys a thing or two."

"Okay," I said. "But first things first. We came here to cliff-dive. Who's ready?"

I looked at the two of them, and all three of us nodded. We were nervous. We were excited. We were right in the middle of one of the wildest nights of our lives.

We walked to the edge of the cliff together and looked down at the water below. It looked so far away, so black and cold, but I knew it would be eighty degrees and perfectly clear once we got in.

TZ took off his shirt and his shoes and looked at us. "Okay, time for you two to strip down."

"As if," Camille said, laughing. "Flan, are you thinking what I'm thinking?"

"Thank God Diane von Furstenberg's couture comes with slip dresses underneath?"

"Exactly!"

We took off our flip-flips and the silky top layers of our dresses. Both of us joined TZ in our little white slips, which covered just enough not to feel totally exposed and embarrassed.

"Okay," TZ said, "you have to make a wish on the way down."

"Says who?" Camille asked.

"Just do it," I said.

"Okay," Camille said. "Here we go!"

We held hands for a second before we jumped, but once we were in the air, we all raised our arms up toward the sky.

It felt like an eternity that I was floating downward toward the water, watching the sun come up. And then, just before I hit the sea, I made my wish.

Please let the rest of this school year be as much fun as tonight, no matter where I end up.

I hit the water.

It was warm and crystal clear, just like I knew it was going to be. Just the way I liked it. I bobbed to the surface and spotted Camille and TZ's heads pop up at the same time. All three of us were laughing and gasping for air.

We couldn't get enough.

Chapter 19

An hour later, after a rigorous backflip contest and attempted relay race between the coves (in which Camille and I beat TZ twice), the three of us parted ways. I dragged my damp, dehydrated self home for some much needed R&R.

Every part of my body felt sore from exertion and exhaustion—but I also felt strangely invigorated. I could feel the endorphins flowing through me, and I remembered that this was what I used to feel like after a really good night out in the city. When you came home too exhausted to stay awake another minute, but too keyed up to actually fall asleep.

I felt like . . . myself again.

I was smiling as I walked up the path to my bungalow, my shoes tucked under my arm.

"Somebody looks like she had a good night last night," a voice said from behind me.

"Aaah!" I screamed, dropping my shoes and causing a family of sleeping toucans to take flight from the palm tree next to me.

I turned around to find Guy, the pool boy and dessert deliverer, who was now dressed in a waiter's suit, standing next to a van and a wheeled cart of trays. He'd thrown up both of his hands in a *Don't shoot* pose when I started yelling.

"You scared me," I said, catching my breath.

"You scared the whole island," he said, laughing a little. "I am sorry for being scary so early this morning."

"What are you doing here?" I asked.

"You didn't order room service?" he said.

"Um, no . . ." I paused. Unless Meredith ordered something. God, I really hoped she wasn't planning on having some breakfast party powwow with Kennedy in my bungalow. All I wanted to do was sleep. Then again, I doubted Meredith would have slept at home last night. According to Kennedy, she couldn't stand to be near me.

I looked at Guy and shrugged. "Sorry," I said. "Maybe the bungalow next door?"

He glanced at a receipt and seemed confused. He looked at the address on our mailbox and then back to the paper in his hand.

"You are Flan?" he asked. "Meredith? You get chocolate chip pancakes and fruit salad for two?"

"Wow," I said, before I even realized I was speaking out loud. "That sounds *good*."

He winked at me. "I think this is for you. Come on, I'll take it inside."

I wasn't going to argue with a man bearing chocolate chip pancakes, so I showed him into the house. He wheeled the cart into the kitchen and unloaded a whole table-scape worth of things more quickly than I would have guessed was humanly possible. Suddenly, there was a brilliant white tablecloth, china service, candlesticks (which he lit), a small bouquet of hyacinths, a small pitcher of OJ, and two covered silver platters at each of the place settings. Guy took a tiny bow, winked at me again, and said, *"Bon appétit."*

And before I could even say thanks, he was gone. He was pretty good at that whole disappearing act thing.

I stared at the banquet before me, wondering where in the world it had come from. Cautiously, I lifted up the lid of the place setting closest to the window. A waft of chocolaty deliciousness came at me, and my mouth watered when I saw the piping hot stack of pancakes. But when I looked more closely at the pancake on the top of the stack, my hand went to my heart.

Someone had spelled out I'M SORRY, FLAN in tiny chocolate chips.

"I really am," a voice said from behind me. "Sorry."

I turned from the table to see Meredith standing in the doorway in her Paul Frank pajamas. She'd taken the braids out of her hair and had tried to tame the kinky mass in a large bun, but strands of crimped brown hair were sticking out all over the place. She looked the way I'd felt for the better part of the trip.

"Did you order this?" I asked her.

She nodded and walked over toward me.

"What happened last night was not something I would have ever wanted to see happen," she said. "Things have just spun so wildly out of control. I feel really badly about the way I acted this week. Do you hate me?"

For a second, I had to think about it. Meredith had been a pretty bad friend this week. But when I tried to see it from her point of view, I realized I hadn't been at my best either. I knew she hadn't joined forces with Kennedy to make me miserable on purpose. She'd been feeling her way through this vacation as much as I had.

"Meredith, I don't hate you. I don't think we'd be up for *Best Week Ever* right now, but I don't hate you."

We sat down at the table. Seeing the food made me forget how tired I was. Suddenly, starvation overtook me, and I couldn't stop staring at the pancakes. But it felt weird to dig in while we were in the middle of an intense conversation.

Luckily, Meredith must have been feeling the same way.

"I'm famished. I haven't eaten since Kennedy and I found these—wait, what am I doing? I'm sorry for bringing that up. I just . . . I don't know when I got so caught up in all this stuff."

Meredith gave me a half smile. I could tell she was still feeling uptight about how rocky things had been.

"So," I said.

"So," she said.

"I guess we should start at the beginning," I said, biting into my first syrupy bite. "What happened to us this week?"

Meredith took her time chewing and swallowing. She took a sip of juice and looked out the window for a moment.

Finally, she said, "You know how Judith and I promised to get over all of our Adam issues before we came on this trip?"

I started to nod my head, when suddenly it hit me that I hadn't thought about Adam in . . . many, many days. Sure, there'd been a lot going on in my head, but how could I have *forgotten* all about him? *That* couldn't be a good sign.

"Flan," Meredith said, looking like she'd been waiting for me to answer. "Remember that?"

"Yeah," I said. "That I do remember."

Remembering my friends' issues with my boyfriend was one thing. Remembering my boyfriend in general . . . hmm.

"Well, I guess it was easier said than done," Meredith said. "But it wasn't just about Adam, you know. It was everything with you. How Judith and I always felt excluded from your life. Like we weren't good enough, or fancy enough, or cool enough to be in the loop about what was going on."

I sighed, because I thought I'd been over this with Meredith a million times before. How many times were she and Judith going to punish me for having a life outside of them?

Meredith was stammering. "I know I should be able to put it behind me, because it seemed like after Adam, you were really trying to be honest, but I just . . . it's taking longer than I'd thought for me to get over it."

"But I don't get it," I said. "You're trying to get over Adam . . . but it feels like you were trying to get back at me by becoming friends with my worst enemy. What kind of friend is that?"

Meredith looked down. "A bad one," she said. "I swear I didn't do it to hurt you—at least not consciously. Kennedy just seemed so cool at first. I thought maybe she'd changed. I mean, how great would it have been if I could help you guys move past your problems with each other?" She fiddled with her napkin and twirled her fork around in her hand. "But then, when it became obvious that you two were never going to be BFF . . . I guess I was already sucked into her web. There's something about Kennedy; she's just so inclusive, and she was always bringing me everywhere with her. We're having so much fun," she said.

We were quiet for a minute, and I tried to get over the fact that Meredith had used the words "inclusive" and "Kennedy" in the same sentence.

"I didn't stop to realize what it was doing to you," she continued. "I always thought you were so self-possessed, that you didn't even need me around. You always seem so in control."

"Meredith," I said, feeling hurt. "Just because someone may *seem* self-possessed doesn't mean she doesn't need her friends to stick by her. It doesn't mean she's okay with being treated like crap."

Meredith nodded. "I know, I know, I can see that now. I was so shocked to see you, you know, all bummed out this week."

"I was pretty shocked to *be* all bummed out this week."

"Kennedy is my friend, too, and I want to keep hanging out with her, but I don't ever want to be the reason that you're upset," she said. "I promise to be more considerate."

I hesitated. Was that good enough?

"Flan?"

"Yeah?"

"What now? Is this going to be another one of those things we say we're going to get over but can't?" Meredith twisted a kinky lock of brown hair around her forefinger, waiting for my response.

"We've only been friends for three months," I said. "I'm just not sure we should have this much baggage yet. It feels like we've spent more time misunderstanding each other and hurting each other's feelings than we've spent having fun."

"That's not good."

"No, it's not," I said, tapping my plate with my fork as I sorted through my thoughts. And then, as things became clearer in my head, I knew that I needed to be really honest with Meredith.

"I'm really glad we're talking all this through," I said. "But I just wonder about us. I've been doing a lot of thinking—about where I fit in, about what will make me the happiest right now—and I know I need to figure out a few more things. But I also know that I don't want to fight with my best friends all the time. It shouldn't be this much of a struggle."

"I think I feel the same way," Meredith said slowly. "I'm so glad that I met you this year, and I'm so glad we got to know each other, but I think we're both starting to feel like we were just—"

"Trying each other on for size?" I finished.

"Exactly," Meredith said. She laughed, but she sounded sad. "And you're this really beautiful Marc Jacobs sweater that I desperately want but that is totally out of my price range."

"And you're the vintage cable-knit cardigan that I'll always admire but could really never pull off."

"This is sad," Meredith said. "I feel like we're breaking up."

"We're not breaking up. We're just starting to understand our friendship for what it is. I still want us to be friends. I hope you do, too."

"I do," Meredith said. She was pushing her fruit salad around on her plate.

"It's better that we recognize this kind of stuff now before we force ourselves back into BFF territory and end up having a huge fight about it."

"You're right," Meredith said. She refilled my OJ glass. "You're always right, Flan. That's another thing about you that totally drives me crazy."

We laughed.

"How about we toast," I said, "to sweaters that we'd love to buy but that really don't match anything else in our closets."

We raised our glasses.

"Cheers," we said at the same time. We smiled at each other, but it was a bittersweet feeling that I couldn't really explain.

Chapter 20

Ladies and gentlemen, the captain has turned off the Fasten Seat Belt sign. The flight attendants will be coming through the cabin with a selection of brunch options."

On Saturday morning, Camille looked over at me from her window seat and frowned. "It's crazy that we're already heading back to the city. Can you believe how fast this vacation flew by?" she asked.

It was funny—there was a time when I thought this was the never-ending vacation from hell, when my stay in Nevis had seemed like an interminable nightmare. But pretty much as soon as I had reconnected with Camille, the trip had been a nonstop blast.

Sitting next to her on the plane, with TZ and Rob passed out in front of us, and Kennedy and Meredith clinging to each other on the other side of the plane, far away from my sphere of recognition . . . I did feel a little bit bummed-out that we were already on our way home.

"No," I said to Camille. "I can't believe it's over."

"At least you'll always have your memories," TZ said in a mocking falsetto voice from in front of us.

Camille and I both kicked his seat. "Shut up, TZ," I said. "Go back to sleep and dream of scratchy necklaces around your whole body."

"Flan, you're killing me," he groaned.

Camille and I giggled and clinked our glasses of sparkling water together. We turned our focus to selecting our brunch options from a touch screen on the front of our seatbacks. Camille ordered the awesome-sounding croissant French toast, and I was toying with the idea of an egg white omelet with spinach.

"I feel like such a heifer after this week. I should probably get something light," I said.

"Like a tasteless, floppy egg white? Whatever, Flan! We're growing girls who are taller than half the boys on this plane. We need our fuel. Plus, we're still technically on vacay. Indulge!"

"Okay, okay. You twisted my arm." I laughed.

Minutes later, the flight attendants brought over two trays of crispy, delicious French toast, with warm maple syrup and fresh strawberries.

"I say we close our eyes and try to pretend we're

still in Nevis," Camille said. "I'll probably be doing that all week. In class, my French teacher will whack me on the head with an eraser like she always does when I zone out."

"Is your French class name still Isobelle?"

"*Oui oui*! And is yours still Madeline?"

"*Bien sur.*"

"We used to have so much fun in French. Remember the day we tried to make crepes, and we got batter all over the slide projector? Madame Virgily was like, '*Psss*, you klutzeee girlzzz! What huzzzband will love you if you cannot make proper crrrepe?'"

Both of us busted out laughing, and then I said, "I really miss having you in my classes."

"Ditto," Camille said. "Obviously you should just drop out of Stuy and come to Thoney!"

"You say that jokingly," I said, "but the truth is, I've been thinking seriously about it. I've already talked about it with my mom."

Camille's eyes got as big as her plate. "*No. Way.*"

"Way. It's not definite yet. I still have some thinking to do. But especially after hanging out with you on this trip, I have to say it's really tempting."

"Wow. Well, I won't try to sway your decision *too* much. I know you have to figure it out for yourself.

But please please please please please come back!"
She grinned. "See, I'm totally staying out of it."

"Part of me wants to," I said. "But what about
Kennedy? Am I up for all that drama and competi-
tiveness again? I don't know."

"Okay, here's the thing," Camille said. She put
down her fork, like whatever she was about to say
would require our full attention. "You know how
everyone is super insecure in middle school?"

"Yeah."

"Well, that's why people like Kennedy can get away
with acting psycho. Most people are followers, and
they'll just do whatever the Queen Bee says. That's
why Miss Mallard's was so painful. That's why *you*
stood out, because you were the only one who'd stand
up to Kennedy."

"I don't know . . . I guess."

"But high school's not like that. It's definitely not
like that at Thoney. I'm telling you, Kennedy's really
not even that cool."

"But she's still so high and mighty."

"She's a little fish in a big pond now. And all the
girls who used to follow her around," she said, raising
her hand sheepishly, "yours truly included . . . well,
everyone's sick of her. None of us sees any reason to

let her boss us around all the time. The whole class is pretty much over it."

"I bet that pisses her off," I said.

"Like you wouldn't believe." Camille laughed. "That's probably why she's gotten even bitchier this year, if that's possible. She's just lashing out and trying to control whatever and whoever she can."

I craned my neck around to see if I could get a peak at Meredith. I could see her chatting away, but I couldn't see Kennedy's face. Then, all of a sudden, Kennedy bolted up from her seat, grabbed her pillow, and started angrily tramping up the aisle.

"Where are you going?" I heard Meredith whine.

"You told me you were going to take a nap for the whole flight," Kennedy said. "You even brought your eye mask. And now you won't shut up for one second. You're driving me effing crazy."

I watched Meredith slump down in her seat and figured that was the end of her run with Kennedy. Bummer—but I wasn't going to say I told her so. At least when she got home, she'd have Judith to return to.

Seeing Meredith look bummed out did make me sad, but it was also really gratifying to glance around the plane and see people buzzing about Kennedy's bitchy outburst.

I turned back to Camille. "So she doesn't rule the school?"

"Absolutely not," Camille said. "In *fact*—"

"Oh, boy," I said. "I know that tone of voice. Do you have an idea?"

"Well, it just so happens that there seems to be a vacancy for who's ruling the ninth grade at Thoney. And I was thinking . . ."

"If I came back . . ."

"It could be you and me!" Camille said.

I thought back to the dream I'd had when we first arrived in Nevis, before I knew half of what was in store for me. How I'd imagined myself walking down the halls at Thoney with girls practically bowing down to me. That had been a funny kind of fantasy, but it wasn't actually what I'd want my life to be like.

I knew then that what I wanted was just to have a tight group of cool friends to go through school with. We didn't have to rule over anyone; we just had to have a good time.

"So ruling the school," I said. "What exactly does that entail?"

"Um, probably something like . . . hanging out with each other every possible second, sharing lots of clothes, planning some non-lame school social functions for a change, ranking at the top of the class, and

having blowout parties with the boys every weekend."

"That sounds like one of your best ideas yet," I
said.

"Told ya," she said.

And once that had been settled, both of us snuggled back in our seats and let a week's worth of
exhaustion overtake us. I didn't wake up until
Camille tapped me on the shoulder to point out the
glittering skyline of New York City out the window
right below us.

"Welcome home," she said. "Now vacation's really
over. We can only deny it for so long."

I watched the city glide below us—the Empire
State Building, the little stacks on stacks of Midtown
buildings, the vast greenness of Central Park—before
we veered east to land at LaGuardia.

"You know what," I said as the plane's wheels
touched back down in our city, "I think we're going to
be okay."

Chapter 21

*B*y the next day, Nevis felt like a slip of a dream. Tucked into bed and listening to Feist drown out the freezing November rain pelting my windows, I found it pretty impossible to believe that only forty-eight hours earlier, I had been diving off a cliff at sunrise.

Now I hunkered down in my room, surrounded by my unpacked suitcase and a whirlwind of papers and books. Every time a burst of thunder rumbled, Noodles would start whimpering and running around in circles like a maniac. I was spending a lot more time calming him down than I was actually studying.

Also, I was keeping pretty busy screening calls from Adam.

Why? What was my problem? We hadn't seen each other in over a week and most people would probably be chomping at the bit to see their S.O. ASAP. But when I got off the plane yesterday and had two messages from him, I suddenly felt a little bit stifled.

> *Hey, Flan, it's Adam. Hope you had a good time on your vacation. Chicago was really cool, too. Anyway, just wanted to see when you're getting back to the city. Give me a call when your plane lands.*

Followed by:

> *Hey, Flan, it's Adam again. I know I just called you, and I know you're still on your flight home. But I just walked by the Fresh store on Bleecker, and they're having a sale, so I thought of you because I know you like their soap and stuff. Anyway, I was hoping we could talk sometime soon. Call me.*

They were such nice, normal messages, but for some reason, I couldn't bring myself to pick up the phone. I'd texted back to say how nice it was of him to call, and that I'd missed him, and that I was tired from the long flight . . . and that I'd give him a call today.

But now it was Sunday night, and he'd left another

message for me this afternoon. I still hadn't returned any of his calls and was feeling increasingly guilty about it. I guess some part of me knew that we needed to have a talk. But I was trying to put it off because at this point, I wasn't sure exactly what to say. How bad of me would it be to just wait to see him at school tomorrow?

"Knock, knock," my dad said, poking his head into my doorway.

"Hey, Dad."

"You two okay up here? I know Noodles is a noodle about thunderstorms."

I lifted my comforter to expose a trembling little fur ball snuggled up against my side. "He's a wimp," I said.

My dad gave Noodles a scratch and then pulled a surprise attack on me: he produced the cordless phone from behind his back.

"Adam's on the phone," he said, covering the mouthpiece. "Said he's been trying to call your cell but thought you might have lost it."

My dad looked across my bed and saw my iPhone sitting right next to me on my pillow. He raised an eyebrow and held out the phone to me.

I took a deep breath and the phone from my dad, who disappeared as quickly as he'd shown up. It was now or never. Maybe when I started talking to him, all the right words would just come to me. Yeah, right.

"Hello?" I said, feeling the same butterflies in my stomach that I'd felt when we first started dating . . . only now I was feeling them for a much less fun reason.

"Hey!" Adam said. "How are you? Good to finally hear your voice. What are you doing?"

"Oh," I said, feeling like a liar before I said a word. "I'm good, not much, you too."

"Me too what?"

"Um, it's good to hear your voice?" I said, like it was a question.

"Oh," he said. "Cool. So how was the trip? Did you guys have a blast?"

It was the first time I'd thought about how I would sum up Nevis in sound-bite form. There was so much to explain that I wasn't sure I'd even be able to get into it all with Adam.

"Yeah," I finally said, "I really did have a blast. How was Chicago?"

"It was a good time. I mostly hung out with my cousins. We just watched a lot of football, talked a lot of football, played a lot of football. How can you go wrong with a lineup like that?"

"Definitely," I said, trying to make my voice sound peppier than I felt. "Sounds awesome."

"So, I was hoping we could see each other soon," he said.

"Well, I'll see you tomorrow in between third and fourth period."

Adam always walked me from English to my gym class because his health class was on the same floor as mine.

"Actually . . . I was wondering, what are you doing tonight?"

"Probably just staying in," I said, wondering if he could tell that I was scrambling to make up an excuse. "I have to get some stuff ready for school tomorrow."

"What if I came over and walked Noodles with you? You have to do that anyway, so I won't be taking up too much of your time, right?"

"Adam, it's pouring out!"

"All the more reason why you shouldn't be out walking him alone. My dad has the world's biggest collection of golf umbrellas. Can I come over in an hour?"

An hour later, I was fastening the Burberry raincoat SBB had bought for Noodles when I first got him. The rain hadn't let up at all, and I was starting to wonder about this plan. Maybe Adam would come to his senses and cancel.

The doorbell rang.

I opened the door and there he was, taking up the whole doorframe and looking great in a Bears hat and a black North Face rain jacket. He held up the biggest umbrella I'd ever seen and produced a Ziploc bag of turkey bacon from his pocket.

"I come prepared," he said, stooping down to give Noodles one of his favorite treats on earth. Noodles jumped into Adam's arms and wagged his tail uncontrollably. Adam held him up and said, "This dog has better fashion sense than half the people at Stuy."

He stood up and we hugged. Adam gave me a quick kiss on the lips.

"Missed you," he said, looking down at the floor. He seemed suddenly shy around me.

I opened my mouth to say something, but a bolt of lightning crashed through the sky, causing Noodles to duck under my legs. The leash got all tangled up around us, and I practically fell into Adam.

"We should probably get going," I said. "Noodles might not last that long out there."

We started walking the usual route, down Perry to Greenwich, and then made a left on Barrow. We ended up right by St. Luke's, my favorite park in the city. But now, with the gates locked and the rain shimmering down in the darkness, it looked kind of forbidding.

"Whoa," Adam said. "This place looks cool." He leaned up against the gate and peaked in. "Have you ever seen this before? It's like a secret garden."

I thought about all the time I'd spent in St. Luke's over the years. The headbands Camille and I had woven out of wildflowers. Or the time when a busload of elderly Italian tourists spooked Noodles, and he got loose and went running for his life right into the park. The first time I'd been kissed.

"Yeah," I said, "I've been here a couple times."

It was just another reminder that Adam and I orbited different spheres. He was perfectly nice, and so considerate, and he was definitely some of the best arm candy at Stuyvesant. But what I was realizing more and more was that arm candy was the last thing I needed.

What I needed was someone who made me want to dive off a cliff. It wasn't specifically about TZ, because I really didn't think of him that way, but there was something exciting about him. It made me realize that I wasn't exactly dating Adam for all the right reasons.

I used to think it was so nice to be able to fall back on the knowledge that this really great guy was into me whenever I got down in the dumps about something. But more and more, I was realizing that I didn't need a guy to fall back on. I had myself, and I had some of the best friends I could imagine if I ever needed something to fall back on. If that was all that Adam was to me, then was it really fair for me to keep pretending we were more?

We looped back around to my brownstone, and Noodles was beyond thrilled to be off his leash and released into my warm, dry apartment. Adam collapsed his colossal umbrella, and the two of us took a seat under the shelter of my stoop. We looked out at the rain.

"So," he said. "You okay?"

"Yeah," I said, but I knew I sounded hesitant.

"What's on your mind?"

I turned to him. "A lot, actually."

"Talk to me." His face looked concerned.

"Well, I've been thinking . . . ." Why was it so hard to say this? "I've been thinking about transferring back to private school. My parents and I have been talking about Thoney."

"Oh," he said. He sounded worried. "I mean, I'd hate to see you go. But I understand that this year hasn't been the easiest for you. I know you have to do what you have to do."

"Really?" I said. I don't know why I was surprised that he was being so supportive.

"Totally. I mean, it's cool seeing you every day and walking you to class and everything, but it's not like you're moving to Yemen. Though separate schools . . . it'll be weird."

He put his arm on my back and started giving me a massage. It was amazing how strong even just one of his hands was.

"I could tell something was weighing you down tonight," he said.

"You could?"

"Yeah, you've been a little withdrawn. But it's understandable. You're going through a lot. At first, I was wondering whether it had to do with us. I don't know, like if your feelings had changed or something. . . ."

For a second, we just looked at each other. It was hard to tell whether he knew what I was going to say next.

"Adam," I said.

He nodded and pursed his lips. "This isn't just about school, is it?"

I shook my head. A tear ran down my cheek. I didn't even know what to say.

"I'm sorry," I whispered.

He rubbed his jaw. "No, I'm sorry, too."

"Why are you sorry?" I asked, confused.

"It's my fault that you feel this way. I mean, I know I get really intense about football. I was thinking about us a lot when I was in Chicago, when I had some space to figure things out. I actually wanted to talk to you tonight, too. I'm not sure this is the best time for either of us to be in a relationship."

"You're not?"

He shook his head.

"Wait, you were going to break up with me, too?"

"I didn't want to; I just worried about us. You know, both of our lives are super busy right now . . . ."

He trailed off.

After a minute, I tried to smile. "I'm going to miss you a lot."

Then he smiled, too. "I know." Then his smile disappeared. "I was worried about having this conversation all weekend. You're a great girl, Flan. I felt lucky when I was with you."

I nodded, knowing that I could return the compliment without telling a lie. Adam was awesome; he just wasn't for me. I put my head up to his neck, and we snuggled for a moment in the rain. "I feel the exact same way about you."

He gave my ponytail a tug. "Friends?" he said.

"Definitely."

Chapter 22

Wait, Flan, *seriously*? You had a *boyfriend* this whole week?"

Camille and I were on the phone late on Sunday night. Even though I knew breaking up with Adam was the right thing to do, I was still feeling pretty bummed about it, so I texted Camille around eleven.

BOY TROUBLE. YOU AWAKE?

She called me back immediately, and when I started to tell her the story about my conversation with Adam, she busted out laughing.

"I'm sorry, it's so not funny. I totally want to be here for you right now. Share your pain with me . . . it's just, I mean . . . you never brought him up *once* the whole trip! And we even talked about boys!"

"It's not funny," I protested. "Okay, it kind of is." Soon, I was laughing, too. "The fact that you never even knew about him, and you and I spent every second together for the past few days, is clearly a sign that I just wasn't that into the relationship."

"Who knew you were so coy? And here I thought you were totally into Rob. He told TZ he thought you were 'breathtaking.' So poetic."

"Oh, God," I said. "Not even."

"He's probably writing girly songs about you this minute."

I sighed. I was still feeling sad and couldn't help but wonder what Adam was doing this minute.

Camille picked up on my pause. "Hey," she said. "I know you're going to be okay, Flan."

"Yeah. I think I just need a break from having a boyfriend for a while," I said.

"I hear you. There are way too many guys for us to have fun with on this island to be tied down right now."

"Sign me up," I said. "When does the fun begin?"

"When's your last final?" she asked.

"Friday morning."

"Me too."

"Okay," I said. "Friday night. My house. Big party."

And this time, when Camille said she'd be there with bells on, I knew that this party would be a vast, vast improvement over the bomb of a party I'd thrown in Nevis.

When I hung up the phone, I heard a knock on my door.

"Flan," my mother said. "What are you doing still awake?"

As I went through the whole story about Adam with my mom, she rubbed my back the way she used to when I was a little girl and couldn't sleep. It never failed to make me feel better about everything from a failed test to a sprained ankle to a lost Tiffany's charm bracelet.

She smiled at me. "You're growing up. And what you did tonight was a very mature thing to do. This is a time of a lot of changes for you, Flan, and I think you're handling yourself just beautifully."

"Thanks, Mom."

"I know something else that will make you feel better," she said. "I had brunch with the dean of Thoney this morning. Everything is all squared away for you to enroll in the spring. You're good to go . . . *if* you decide that's what you want."

As all the ups and downs of the past week flew through my mind, I suddenly realized that a lot of the ups had to do with things at Thoney, and a lot of the downs were things I could leave behind at Stuy. At first, I'd been so reluctant, because I didn't want to feel like I was quitting. But now, I didn't feel like that at all. I just felt like I had a much better understanding of what it was that was going to make me happy.

I smiled at my mom. "I'm glad I gave Stuy a try this fall. But Thoney is starting to seem like a better fit."

"Phew," my mother said. "And I thought I was going to have to bust out all my old yearbooks to convince you of all that Thoney has to offer."

I laughed.

"I think we need to celebrate," my mom said. "What would you say to a big old-fashioned family party here on Friday night? Would that put a cramp in your social schedule?"

Sometimes my mom is so awesome—and so clairvoyant.

"I think I could fit it in," I said, laughing.

As the week went by, it became clear that there were a lot more things to celebrate than just my decision about school. For one thing, as Camille reminded me, I was single and fabulous. And I had already completed four of my finals and aced them—even Algebra, which could have been my downfall. On top of that, Patch finally got around to opening his Princeton letter, and (surprise surprise) he got accepted early. Emerald Wilcox had been sleeping in our guest room all week—she and Feb were planning on redecorating the house—and her half birthday was coming up on Friday. And, as if all that weren't enough, my father had just closed the deal on the massive bungalow my parents had stayed in while we were in Nevis.

A huge bash was definitely in order.

Emerald and Feb had taken it upon themselves to organize and execute the Half Birthday/ Congratulations/Good Luck/Nevis Forever party of the century. Originally, my mom had hired Harrison & Shriftman to plan the party, but when Emerald and Feb produced résumés to show her their mounds of event-planning experience, she had to agree to hire them.

To their credit, they did put in a lot of hours to ensure that the party would be a success. But all week, our kitchen looked like a war zone. I decided to hole myself up in my room to escape it and to cram for my last two finals, so I could enter Thoney with a respectable high school transcript.

During study breaks, when I'd wander down into the kitchen for some mac and cheese and Fresca, I had to weed through all sorts of floor plans and light fixtures and even a giant box of glittering

Judith Leiber piñatas just to find my way to the fridge.

By Friday night, my house was totally decked out. Emerald and Feb had organized each different fete in a different room of the house and given each one a different thematic seasonal twist.

For Patch, the future college freshman, they'd decked out the living room with autumnal Back to School décor.

For Emerald's half birthday party, the kitchen was in full springtime bloom—a shout-out to her real birthday in May.

My parents' new property acquisition in Nevis was a Summer Lovin' theme in the greenhouse on our roof (partially to keep the adults' party separate from the kids' party down below).

And last but not least, I was given winter, for the season when I'd be entering Thoney. Emerald and Feb had set up heat lamps along our back patio and strung twinkling white Christmas lights all over the place. Feb helped me pick out a sparkling silver slip dress and apply matching eye shadow to my lids. A giant diamond snowflake piñata hung overhead.

Everything was perfect. I sat down on one of the silver swings Emerald had strung from the trees in the yard. I could hear the various parties inside beginning to buzz, but so far none of my friends had shown up. I pumped my legs lightly and began to swing. I was thinking about whether I felt really grown-up right now or very much like a kid. As the baby of the family, it was no new feeling to be the youngest at the party, but the last few weeks had been such a time of transition and growing up that I also felt really mature.

So much had changed. I no longer felt like I needed to have Adam to fall back on—or any guy for that matter. Kennedy Pearson was a threat to me no more. I'd finally come to terms with the fact that there was no sense in forcing a best friendship with Meredith and Judith, when it was mostly making all three of us miserable. And perhaps most surprisingly, I wasn't at all paranoid that no one would come to my party tonight. I'd lived through party throwing hell once already this week, and here I was. I'd survived.

Just after eight o'clock, my first guest stepped out into the yard: Camille. She was wearing a black halter dress, and her long, long dirty blond hair was swept to the side in a loose braid. When she stepped out into our backyard, her jaw dropped.

"Whoa! Hello, Snow Queen," she said.

"Welcome to the Winter Wonderland," I said, standing up to give her a kiss.

"This party rocks . . . but I'm a little confused," she said. "I just narrowly avoided being forced into a keg stand by Patch in your foyer. And why was Emerald blowing out candles on only half of a cake?"

I laughed. "Feb was the mastermind behind this shindig."

"Say no more," Camille said, picking up a bubble wand that blew bubbles in the shape of snowflakes. "So what are we celebrating this season? Your singleness and fabulosity, I'm guessing?"

I paused when I realized I still hadn't told Camille that I'd signed the final paperwork to enroll at Thoney this morning.

I pointed to the ice sculpture in the middle of the garden, which Feb had had engraved with BYE BYE STUY, OLÉ THONEY.

Camille looked over at me with a huge grin on her face.

"You decided?"

"I decided!" I yelled, matching the expression on her face.

The next thing I knew, Camille had slung herself around me, and we were spinning in a circle around the backyard.

"This is the best news I've heard since I found out Pinkberry was coming to the city!"

We laughed and hugged some more.

"So, this is where the party is!"

I turned around to find TZ coming down the steps. He was decked out in a Ferragamo sweater and was accompanied by a nicely dressed crew of guys—including Danny, whom I almost didn't recognize because his muscles were covered up by a sweater; Rob, who I almost didn't recognize without his guitar looped over his shoulder; and Alex Altfest, who I definitely *did* recognize, especially when he gave me a tight squeeze and whispered in my ear, "I was wondering when you'd invite me to one of your famous parties."

I wanted to do something cute and coy like wink at him or give him a witty comeback, but all I managed to do was turn beet-red and say, "I'm glad you're here."

When I'd recovered from my blushing incident with Alex, I turned around and realized, to my pleasant surprise, that the entire yard had filled up with my friends.

"Flan's coming to Thoney! Flan's coming to Thoney!" Camille shouted to anyone who would listen. She was practically doing cartwheels as she raced around the party to tell every single person she could find.

"Good news travels fast," TZ said. "Looks like you have a lot to look forward to."

"If your social life at Thoney is anything like this party, I would say you do," Rob agreed.

I looked around the party that had formed around me and thought about how right everything had felt about my decision to switch schools. I'd invited both Meredith and Judith to come tonight, but both of them had already left town for Christmas break. I wasn't exactly sure what the future would hold for the three of us—there might not be any more Boy Circles in our near future, but I knew that I would definitely make an effort to keep in touch. Maybe having a little bit of space would be a good thing for our threesome.

But for now, I could just kick back and revel in the fact that the music was pumping, the lighting was perfect, and everyone was laughing and having an awesome time. I had to hand it to Feb and Emerald; this party put my Nevis party to shame.

"Having fun?" Feb said, coming up from behind me.

I put my arm around her, and we looked out at the revelers below. "Thank you so much, Feb. I'm having an awesome time."

"Don't thank me. I just bossed some people around and hit the clearance aisle at pinatas.com."

"Yeah, but my last party was nowhere near as—"

"Don't be so modest, Flan. This party's awesome because you have a ton of friends who want to celebrate with you." She squeezed my hand. "Don't ever tell Emerald I said this," she said. "But some of her guests have been spotted sneaking out here. Apparently the vibe is just a lot more chill."

"Obviously," I laughed. "It *is* winter."

"Yeah, right," she said, giving me a wink. "You know it's you."

The next day, SBB called me early in the morning. The crew had just finished wrapping up the *Bonnie and Clyde* set, and she was flying back from Texas.

"First things first," she said. "I must stop by to check in on my steamer trunk. I've been such a neglectful mother."

When we left Nevis, I'd had her trunk shipped back in cargo, and it had been sitting in my dad's parking spot in the covered garage across the street ever since. Talking on the phone with Sara-Beth, I could look out our library window and see the massive thing sitting like sunken treasure in between two Beamers.

A couple of our neighbors were circling it, probably wondering whether they were seeing things—just like I'd been wondering when I first saw it come off the plane on the beach. Now I noticed that my neighbor's two twin daughters were beginning to climb up the sides of the trunk as if it were playground equipment. SBB would definitely not like grimy two-year-old handprints on her precious happy place.

"Um, why don't you swing by my place on your way back from the airport?" I suggested.

When SBB arrived at my place, she looked even more energized than normal. She'd had really short bangs cut bluntly across her forehead and was wearing all black except for her hot pink snow boots.

"How's my baby?" she asked me, plopping down on the leather couch in my living room.

"I'm good, thanks," I said. "But I do wish you'd been in town last night. We had the sweetest—"

"Not you, Flan, sorry," she said. "My happy place. I just want to make sure it's still in one piece."

"Oh," I said, laughing and sitting down next to her. "Yep, it survived the trip. That trunk was a lifesaver, SBB. Thank you so much for the loan."

"*Phew,*" she said. "I was a little concerned. I know what you did when you were entrusted with a frog in Bio last month. I didn't want you releasing my trunk back into the wild."

"No danger of that," I said. But I had to admit, I was a little surprised SBB hadn't asked me about the rest of the trip. I'd been in pretty rare form the last time she'd seen me.

"What's that face?" she said. "Chin up, frowny, you'll get wrinkles." She put two fingers around the corners of my mouth and turned my lips up. "What do you think," she said, "that I'm putting my trunk before you?"

"No . . . . I don't know . . ."

"*Flan*, I knew *you* were fine the rest of the week." She rubbed her hands together conspiratorially. "I had a spy in Nevis."

"What do you mean, you had a spy?" I said.

"Don't you remember Guy?" she said. "You know, the pool guy? I had him report back to me via e-mail every day to discuss how you were doing. I didn't want to be overbearing and bug you all the time, but I was worried about you. I wanted to make sure you were okay."

"So you hired the pool guy to spy on me?"

"More or less, yes," she said with a shrug, like this was a completely normal thing to do.

"Wait, were you behind the apology pancakes from Meredith?" I asked. Suddenly, everything that happened on the trip seemed to have a double SBB meaning.

"Not entirely," she said. "But Guy did tell me that your friend Meredith wanted to spell out her 'I'm sorry' in parsley on top of an omelet. That's when I interfered. Obviously I knew you'd prefer chocolate chip pancakes!"

"I can't believe this," I said.

"No biggie. And anyway, when I heard Camille was in town, I was able to lay off a little bit. I knew you'd forget about all the drama and just have a blast. Rumor has it that girl's got it going on."

"SBB, you're too much," I said, hitting her lightly with a pillow.

"I'll tell you who's too much," she said, fending off my attack. "Jake freaking Riverdale."

"Uh-oh," I said. "Don't tell me he's still being a total micromanaging control freak."

"Um, actually . . . there's some news I should probably spill," she said. "Hold on." She took out her keys. "Let's go get into my trunk before I dish the whole story."

We walked outside and crossed the street. Once we made it inside the garage, I glanced around to make sure no one else was there, knowing how crazy we'd look to any of my neighbors if they caught us lounging in a steamer trunk with the disco ball.

But then, my intrigue over the Jake Riverdale story outweighed any anxiety about being taken for a crazy person, so I climbed in next to SBB.

"Okay," I said. "Spill."

"Well," she said, squirming a little. "JR and I . . . well, we kind of . . . fell in love on the set."

"Excuse me?" I said.

"It's true!" she said, throwing out her arms in a big open shrug. "But don't worry; I already told him I'm keeping my name."

"Oh," I laughed. "*Phew*."

She nodded gravely. "Sara-Beth Benny isn't just a name anymore, after all. It's a brand-now, too. Did I tell you I'm starting my own perfume line?"

"Hold on, back up. Perfume talk in a minute. First, I need to know all the details about you and Jake Riverdale. How did you get together? When did you two stop drinking the Haterade? What about your hot pilot from Nevis?"

"Oh, Luke's ancient history! And with JR, it was a whirlwind of things. The south was just such a perfect background for a romance. We'd go line dancing every night and, you know, one thing led to another, and suddenly, we were mugging down. That's how they say 'making out' in the south."

"You lost me at 'line dancing.'" I said, shaking my head.

"Love makes you do crazy things," she said. "Anyway, it's all so new, and I really don't want to jinx it."

Her eyes darted from side to side. "Or let a single detail leak to the press." Her voice dropped to a whisper. "So, let's change the subject. Tell me more about your trip. Our darling espionager only picked up on so much, being male and all."

"Okay," I said. "Here goes."

As we settled back against the Murphy Bed, I delved into the whole trajectory of the trip—from good, to bad, to worse, to borderline agonizing, and then finally to totally awesome.

"Hmm," SBB said when I was all talked out. "This TZ character. Very interesting development. Guy sent me a picture of him from his cell phone, but it was too blurry for me to make out any good details."

"SBB, I cannot believe your stalking tendencies! I'm surprised at you. And I feel slightly violated."

"Oh, please," she said, shrugging off my surprise with a wave of her hand. "I have paparazzi on me at all hours, and I've lived to tell the tale. You can handle it for three days. Plus, I only had your best interest at heart."

"Okay, but can this be the last time you hire foreign men to spy on me?" I asked.

"Deal," she nodded. "I'll even make it up to you with brunch. My treat."

I hadn't realized how hungry I was until she mentioned brunch. "Great idea," I said, standing up. "Where should we go?"

"Sit down," she said, giving my shirt a yank. "We'll have it delivered here from EJ's. It'll be like breakfast in bed!"

Thirty minutes and a strange look from the delivery guy later, we spread the food out in front of us. SBB nibbled on her egg white omelet and stole several large bites of my Belgian waffle.

"So after everything you went through on this trip," she said, "do you feel like you had your happy ending?"

I nodded. "And now I think I'm going to have a happy beginning."

"What do you mean?"

I paused. I knew SBB wouldn't judge me, but I was still getting used to telling people about Thoney. Finally, I swallowed my waffle and my hesitation and said, "I decided to transfer schools again. Stuy was a good experience, but I guess I am a private school girl after all."

SBB's eyes lit up. "You know what," she said, "I had a dream the other night that you were going to Thoney and were totally ruling the school. *Weird.*"

"Was Zac Efron in it, by any chance?"

"No, Flan, it wasn't *that* kind of dream. Sorry." She laughed.

"So do you think I'm making the right choice?" I asked her.

"Absolutely." She nodded. "After we finished shooting, JR and I took a few days off and went down to Savannah to veg out. And that was when I realized that falling for him was the right decision. Just like you with school. Sometimes, I think all you need is a vacation to clear your head and show you what it is you really want."

"Are you equating your desire for JR with my desire to have an easier time in high school?" I said, shaking my head at her.

"*Shhh,*" she said, practically covering my mouth with her hand. "I swear I just saw that sleazy tabloid reporter from *AM New York*. We're not supposed to leak the details of our love to the press until a week before the premiere."

"Sorry," I said, even though I was pretty sure that the person she saw was just Mrs. Kelmer, the oldest tenant on our street, who'd lived in the same brownstone for the last eighty-five years.

"Anyway," SBB said, recomposing herself, "I know you're going to have a better time at Thoney. But I must warn you. High school is hell wherever you are. I'm sure there will be some haute drama going down there, too. But of course, none that you won't be able to handle."

"I know, you're right," I said. "I'm not trying to run away from anything difficult. I'm just trying to find the right fit."

"Omigod. Speaking of the right fit," SBB said. "I must take you home with me right now."

"Why's that? Is Jake lounging around in tight-fitting pants?"

"Better! Okay, maybe not better. But I just got a shipment from Zac Posen. His new line is ready and not a single piece in the collection fits me. Can you believe it? It's torture. I do hate you for being so tall, but I can't stand to see so much good couture go to waste."

"Are you suggesting what I think you're suggesting?" I said.

SBB stood up, whisked the remnants of our brunch into a trash bag, and closed the happy place for business.

"You *do* have a first day of school coming up, don't you?" she said. "And let's face it, this *is* Thoney. You're going to have to look seriously chic if you plan to rule *that* school."

"I don't know about ruling the school," I said. "Let's just aim for being happy there."

"Flan," she said, putting her arm around me and leading me back to her brownstone. "Don't under-estimate the clairvoyant power of my dreams. If I say you're going to rule the school, you're going to rule the school. Now come on—let's see if Zac sent any extra long pairs of pants!"

I just laughed and followed her inside. I was so lucky to have a best friend who fit me perfectly.

Can't wait to find out what happens with
your favorite Inside Girl?

Turn the page for a sneak peek of
ALL THAT GLITTERS,
the fourth book in the Inside Girl series.

$\mathcal{R}$epeat after me," SBB said. She was sitting half-in and half-out of a pair of Gucci riding pants with her eyes closed and her hand placed over her heart. "I, Sara-Beth Benny."

Camille and I gave each other a sly grin. We were standing in a private dressing room on the fifth floor of Bergdorf Goodman on 58th Street, surrounded by champagne flutes of Pellegrino and a tray of chocolate-covered strawberries the shopgirl had brought in. We were waiting for her to return with the wheeled rack of winter clothes for some back-to-school shopping, and in the meantime, SBB was making us vocalize our New Year's resolutions.

"Wait," Camille said, nudging me and giggling. "If it's *your* resolution, why do we repeat after you? We're not Sara-Beth Benny, last time I checked."

SBB opened one eye and looked at Camille. "Collective affirmation of resolutions has the highest rate of follow-through." She pinched Camille playfully on the arm. "Don't worry—we'll get to you guys next."

As someone who was used to indulging SBB's crazy ways, I gave Camille a nod and joined SBB on the gilded carpet. Camille plopped down next to me, and we followed Sara-Beth's instructions:

"I, Sara-Beth Benny," we repeated, as mock-solemnly as we could.

In the three-way mirror in front of us, I could see our reflections from all angles. Camille was still glowing from her family's New Year's trip to Cabo, and SBB looked fresh faced from a week off of filming and a week on with her new boyfriend, actor-musician Jake Riverdale.

As I looked up at my reflection, I was pleased to see that I had my own sort of glow. It wasn't from a vacation tan, and it wasn't from a boy, but it was satisfying in a very Flan way. It had to do with my decision to return to Thoney this semester, and even though my excitement was tinged with a case of nerves, I was happy.

SBB continued. "I, Sara-Beth Benny, promise to donate a portion of all of my movie and TV royalties, as well as my perfume line profits, to help those in Africa who are less fortunate than I. And maybe to adopt a child who needs love and who I could cart around in one of those cute Karma Baby slings. And to grow at least six inches by July."

"Whoa," Camille said. "I was just going to try to start recycling more."

Just then, the salesgirl returned, wheeling in a giant clothing rack full of gorgeous-looking sweaters, pants, and slinky dresses. Instantly, we forgot our collective New Year's affirmation and pounced on the clothes like wild animals.

"Omigod," SBB said, grabbing a sheer polka-dotted dress from the middle of the rack. "Is this so 'Flan on the first day of school' or what?"

I held up the tiny Geren Ford dress to my body. It was asymmetrical, and tied around the left shoulder with an almost nonexistent green silk strap. It barely covered my hips.

"It's cute," I said, stalling to find the right words so I wouldn't offend SBB. "But it looks more like 'Flan gets thrown out of school before third period.'" My hand reached for a supercozy navy Autumn Cashmere drape sweater. "How about something more like this?" I said.

"Okay, Mister Rogers," Camille said, taking it from my hands and hanging it back up. "Believe me, I know that rocking the five-foot-ten frame does present its own set of fashion challenges, but I will not let you be Frump Master on the first day of school." She rooted through the rack of clothes and pulled out a shrunken gray blazer with three-quarter sleeves and a really unique notched collar. "How about something like this?"

"*Cute*!" SBB and I said simultaneously.

"Ooh," SBB continued, looking at the label. "And it's my old costar Waverly James's new line. She was showing me how to wear this . . . there are these really cute leggings that go with it. . . ." Her voice trailed off as her tiny body virtually disappeared into the rack of clothes.

"SBB," I said, sticking my head in after her. "Are you still in here?"

"Ta-da!" She jumped out, holding a pair of stretchy black leggings with a row of brass studs around the ankles. She waggled them at me. "Terrick Zumberg, here you come!"

Camille squealed. "Um, speaking of New Year's

resolutions! Flan, you *must* wear those leggings with this blazer on the first day of school. Because you know what happens on the first night of school, right?"

I shook my head. "Homework?" I asked hesitantly.

"No! All the Thoney girls go to David Burke's to meet the Dalton boys for pizza—and then TZ will see you in *this*!"

I let my friends hold up the clothes against me and looked at myself in the mirror. The ensemble was totally my style, but I was suddenly feeling a little overwhelmed. It made me nervous that Camille just assumed I'd be up on all the Thoney protocol. And now there were all these expectations about impressing TZ, whom I'd barely seen since we'd hung out over Thanksgiving break in Nevis. The old fears that I thought I'd rid myself of were creeping back into my mind. What if I couldn't keep up?

Camille must have sensed me getting tense. "Hey," she said, linking her arm through mine. "Don't stress. This semester is going to be amazing, whether or not you decide to grace TZ with your affection."

I looked in the mirror at my two best friends and nodded. "You're right. Thoney—and David Burke's pizza party—bring it on."

"Of course Camille is right," SBB agreed. "Now try these on so I can envy your long legs even more."

I slipped into the leggings, and Camille handed me a long ribbed cotton tank with detailed stitching that fell well below my waist. When I pulled the blazer on over it and looked in the mirror, I felt instantly more self-assured. I guess I did look pretty good.

"Hey, you guys," SBB called. She'd snuck out of the dressing room and was standing at the edge of the shoe department, holding up a pair of Joie patent leather Mary Janes in one hand and a pair of caramel-colored Michael Kors boots in the other. "Flan, come here and try these on with that outfit."

Camille and I left the dressing room and stepped out into the bright, bustling floor of the shoe department. The Mary Janes were adorable.

"Ooh," Camille said, holding one up to me and putting on a dramatic advertising voice. "This shoe will take you from study hall to evening ball."

"And right into the arms of *TZ*," SBB sang.

"*Shhh*!" I blushed and immediately looked around. It would be just my luck that TZ's cousin or grandmother would be shopping within earshot. Luckily, there were just the usual crew of personal assistants on their BlackBerrys and a few overbearing Upper East Side mothers making their daughters try on "just one more pair" of Chloé loafers.

But then . . .

"I *thought* I recognized those voices," said a voice from behind me.

I spun around and realized I hadn't been comprehensive enough in my coast-is-clear sweep of the store. Standing before me was my ex-best friend, Kennedy Pearson.

"I was just picking up my outfit for the first day of spring semester, and I couldn't help but overhear your little discussion in the dressing room."

I looked at Kennedy's clear plastic Bergdorf garment bag and was stunned to see the very same pair of black leggings I had on. I could feel the blood rushing to my face. If I was being honest with myself, Kennedy was the biggest reason why I couldn't shake off my nerves about school.

She put her hand on my arm. "I just wanted to apologize, Flan."

"For what?" I said, moving my arm from her grasp. "For eavesdropping?" *For stealing my outfit? For being the devil incarnate?*

"No," she winced dramatically. "For having to be the one to tell you, when it's clear that you're really into TZ." She covered her face with her hand in faux-anguish. "How do I say this? I'm so sorry, Flan, but TZ and I are sort of together. As of New Year's."

There was a time when I wouldn't have known how to respond to this. A time when my face would have turned red, and I would have had some whiny, embarrassing response like, "But I thought he liked *me*." In that moment, standing under the soft Bergdorf lights, it became so clear that neither Kennedy nor TZ was worth the heartache.

"You know what, Kennedy? You can have him. He's flaky and you're pathetic. You two deserve each other."

Kennedy's face flushed bright red, and her glossy lips parted in shock.

"Wow, go Flan!" Camille whispered at my side.

Just as I was reveling in the fact that I had finally said the right thing at the right time, Kennedy's cell phone started to ring.

"Oh," she said, "that's TZ now." Putting the phone to her ear, she said, "Hold on a sec, honey." Then she turned back to me. "You know, Flan, some people might think you're 'brave' to come back to Thoney, but I personally think you're really, *really* going to regret it. Especially after that precious jealousy outburst you just had." Waving her leggings in my direction, she started toward the elevator. "Can't wait to see you Monday!"

"Oh, she's *going* to see you Monday," SBB shouted, hurling a wad of tissue paper from a nearby shoebox at Kennedy's receding back.

My legs started shaking in my studded leggings, and I grabbed Camille's and Sara-Beth's arms for support. I swallowed hard. This was *not* the fabulous start I'd envisioned for my new year.

What had I gotten myself into?

Find out what happens when Flan
heads back to Thoney in . . .
ALL THAT GLITTERS
an Inside Girl novel
Coming September 2008